MW01515408

GRAYSON

This is Our Life Series

F.G. Adams

Cover Design & Photography:
Bre Clark Photography

Model:
Benjamin Bartholomew

Interior Design:
Daryl Banner

Editor:
Julia Goda

Proofer:
CJ Fling

Dedicated to all the men and women

serving our country at home and abroad.

Thank you for your service.

CONTENTS

PROLOGUE

Running as fast as my short legs allow through the dense canopy of oak trees, I dodge the thick underbrush on our ranch. I'm almost to the moon-shaped windowed door of the enormous two-story log home we live in. I hear a thundering roar and cringe from the movement coming directly over the hill off to the left.

I push the heavy wooden door open, shuffling through before it slams shut behind me almost like a beacon bringing in ships. Languidly, yet as stealthily as a seven-year-old boy can be, I run down the hall to find my hiding spot. *If I make it there, I might be safe.*

If I'm quiet and don't move, maybe he won't hear me, won't find me. I'm so scared. My fear is tangible. I can taste it all around me. *Why did I go outside? Why didn't I listen? Bump, Crash*! I hear the sounds getting closer. *I hope he doesn't find me.* I curl up in a tight ball in the corner of the closet as I wait for the inevitable.

My thoughts begin to wander, thinking about my four sisters. My older sisters, Fallyn, Jo, and Sage, left me and my baby sister, Adalyn, who's small and helpless. I have to protect her. At all costs. Surely this is why? The reasons they all fled this house. And one day I will too.

My head hurts, and the scratches on my legs from the barbed wire fence are slowly bleeding and pooling on the floor below. Sweat is trickling down my back from running so hard outside on this warm summer day. It's quiet. *Please don't find me.* Maybe I can rest now, drift off for a few minutes, hours, seconds...time really isn't relevant for me at my age.

My thoughts are interrupted when the sturdy door of my secret security closet swings open. *BAM!*

"There you are. I told you if you ran, it would be worse. You asked for it," a gruff, colossal voice yells.

Standing before me is the monster from my nightmares, my father. He's so big compared to me. He is looming over me dressed in overalls, wearing his Stetson, and holding his token of choice, the leather belt. My fear escalates, and black spots overtake my vision.

"Please don't, I'm sorry, sir!" I holler.

I'm caught. Grabbed by my shirt and yanked out of the closet, there is nowhere left to run. Struggling to escape, I twist my body from left to right, violently flailing my arms and kicking my legs. Praying to escape this nightmare before it begins.

"Please, don't, I'm sorry, sir!" I scream at the top of my lungs.

I'm thrown across the room, and my body collides with the adjoining wall. A picture falls and glass shatters all around me, cutting my arms. Little drops of blood form from the openings on my flesh. In slow motion, my arm is grabbed, and I'm hauled back toward my bed. Trying to find traction to stand, I slip and fall backwards, slamming into the lamp on the nightstand.

My Ninja Turtle lamp succumbs to his fury, too, as it bursts into small pieces. Scrambling free, I rush toward the door, trying to bypass his long reaching arms once more. Only a few more feet and I can run.

"Please don't, I'm sorry, sir!" I howl, hoping against all hopes that my plea reaches out to the angels, but my prayers won't be answered today. They never are.

That's when I feel the sting of the frayed leather strap as it bites against my back through my clothes, shredding my tender skin. Welts are instant. Blood is what he requires to sate his demented craving. His anger is palpable. It feeds his monster. The monster his father created in him. Passed from father to son. From generation to generation.

This is going to be really bad. My pleading and cries go unnoticed with every painstaking slash, swing, and the onslaught of punishment begins. It will all be over soon enough, but *I have to endure*, I must take it, to keep my baby sister safe. That's when I retreat into that safe place in my consciousness that stays untouched...even by him.

CHAPTER 1
GRAYSON

Ten years later.

Waking from another bout of my father's glorious learning exercises, I see mother is sitting quietly in the corner, staring out into the darkness, singing while rocking sweet little Addie. "*Amazing Grace. How sweet the sound. That saved a wretch like me....*"

Even though Addie is ten now, mom loves to hold and rock her, and Addie seems to enjoy the attention. It's a place of peace for mom, a reprieve she gets so little.

Being the fourth child out of five, the only boy at that, my protective instincts kicked in when I was younger. I fiercely protect my mom and baby sister, even when the consequences have nearly killed me a time or two. *It's my job to protect them.*

Her face contorts in pain when she notices me watching her. I can tell once again she tried to intervene, and now her body bears the consequences.

"You shouldn't have tried to stop him. You knew he'd use you as his punching bag. He's done it before. I can handle it. You're fragile, mom. Why'd you do that?"

"Grayson, my dear sweet son, what kind of mother

would I be if I hadn't? He wasn't going to stop this time," she replies.

Knowing she's right, and as much as I try to remember why I have to be strong, I'm not Superman. I'm fighting a battle against Goliath, and I'm the pion he's about to squish. My father gets this way all the time. His *normal* persona is viewed only by family. It can be the slight closing of a door, walking down the hallway too fast, or maybe just chewing my food the wrong way that sets him off. This has been happening for years.

My oldest sister, Fallyn, left home when she was sixteen; and she is finally happy. No thanks to dear ole dad. He tried to control her, but she had too much of grandma's stubbornness inside her to give up. Talk about a war...my sister not only won the battle, she escaped hell and his grip. But I was just a baby when all that went down. The other two, Jo and Sage, their stories are a little different, but the end result is the same. They're gone too. Released from this giant chasm of hell. *Home sweet home.*

Looking over at mom, I can't help but wonder why she stays. She's beautiful and intelligent. She is a great teacher and loves her job. We could leave. She could take Addie and I far, far away, and we could live without the fear of making a wrong move, but she won't! *Please, mom, tell me why?* I've asked this question so many times, and she always shakes her head and gives me a lopsided smile. She will never leave him. She doesn't know how. Mom truly loves the monster she shares her life with.

"Don't worry, momma, this will be gone in a few weeks. I can hide it and no one will know. Let's just forget it happened," I quietly murmur. She cringes and barely nods.

Subconsciously, she knows I speak the truth. This isn't the first time he's lost his temper over nothing. When I was younger, it was worse, but as my body grew and he aged, the pain wasn't as intense. Don't get me wrong, it still hurts like a son of a bitch, but I've learned to garner that pain and turn it into something productive. My own personal vengeance. I will never be the rancher he wants.

Slowly but surely as my sisters returned to Lakeview, it's helped rein in his fits of anger. My father is aware of their presence and won't act out while they are around. In their own way, they are protecting us. Ensuring he walks the line...straight and narrow. Addie is the one who's benefited the most from their presence. He's never touched her in anger, and they won't allow him to. *Thank God.*

My father's abusive nature was bred from his father's. It's a dirty secret the infamous Blackwood family has tried to contain, and only a few have witnessed the brutality. He's a well-respected deacon in the church, rubs noses with politicians around the State, and sits on several committees for some of the wealthiest businessmen in the Panhandle. *Shit! He's one of those wealthy men!* Looking in from the outside, he is the perfect husband and father.

"I love you, my sweet boy," mom whispers. Standing with difficulty, she takes Addie by the hand and leaves my room.

I'm left feeling bereft. My body is on fire as a constant reminder of what started this mess. Earlier, we were all sitting around the dining room table eating dinner. Mom had made the best chicken potpie, and I was on my second helping when I casually mentioned my intention to apply to West Point. That was the moment his fist flew across the table and connected with my body. Dishes crashed to the floor along with me. From there it escalated to his favorite leather belt and several unwanted bruises along my back and torso.

How would I know that he had other plans for furthering my education? He's never before called attention to where I should go. That's the problem. He never asks me anything. When he decides it's time for whatever he has concocted in his head, I'm told what to do and how to do it. Some things never change.

The next morning, I'm woken to the light blaring in my eyes and my father fiercely shaking me. In an unconscious moment, I move quickly, escaping his reach. Years of practice and know-how have taught me that maneuver. Sleeping lightly is the other. I'm on the other side of my bed, using it as a barrier between us. Trusting my instincts to keep me from harm and out of his reach.

GRAYSON
(This Is Our Life #1)

"Grayson, you're making us late, and I need to leave here in the next five minutes!" my father yells as he exits my room. It's his usual demeanor. *You can't change the spots on a leopard,* I'm told.

I remind him as he retreats down the hallway, "I have ROTC practice today, sir." He mumbles his disgust as his heavy footsteps retreat down the hall. My whispered hope is that he'll leave and I can drive my truck today. *One can always hope.*

Another day in the life of Grayson Blackwood. Stumbling into my bathroom, I jump in the shower and get ready for school. School. It's the only venue I have to express myself. I'm not an artist. Couldn't draw stick figures. No artistic talent here. Although each member of my family is musically gifted in one way or another. My talent lies with a six-string guitar.

Just one more year, I tell myself, *one more year until I can leave this wretched house and never return to Lakeview, Florida*, I vow to myself as the water washes away all of the filth from the day before, washes it away down the drain along with my free will. For now, I have to bide my time. Just like my older sisters, I'll make it out. I have to.

CHAPTER 2

Ella

"I'm coming, just a minute!" I yell through the stuffy little house. I finish my makeup, then with one more glance in the mirror at the image staring back at me, I'm ready for whatever the day holds.

My family and I live in a cramped, insignificant dwelling with nondescript white siding and blue trim. The front porch has just enough room for my mom's favorite pastime, her rocking chair. It's one of the few moments of peace in her existence from the disease that cripples her body. She enjoys gazing at the small flowerbed with pink azaleas in the front yard. The yard has been neglected for weeks. Not to mention, it's in a really poor, unnerving part of town close to the railroad tracks. Just like my dad craves. The more we blend in with the natives, the less attention we attract. He's the reason we are here.

"Sure thing, Ella honey. Hurry up 'cause you're going to be late!" my mom hollers back from the kitchen.

This is my usual morning. Wake up, fix breakfast for everyone, and then hurry up and get dressed in enough time to leave for school, but not before making sure that my little brother is getting ready and on his way as well. I guess I should be thankful, and really, I am, but it's just that sometimes I wish I didn't have to take care of *everything* that goes on in our house.

You see, that's my life. I'm sixteen years old with all the responsibilities of most grown-ups. My parents, well, they aren't really what you'd call typical parents. Mom is sick and has been for a long while now. They'd called it terminal years ago, but by the grace of God, she's still with us. However, it's only a matter of time before her roll is called. I pray every night that God will let her stay with us just a little longer, and so far, He's answered my prayers. She just can't help out in the normal ways a mother should or could. But that's alright, because one more day with her is worth all of it.

Then there's my dad. Well...he's a grifter of sorts, a con artist. That's what brought us to this little town here in Florida two years ago. He was once again running away from another con, another fella he wronged. Lately, he's started dabbling in drugs. He keeps telling me it's not true, but I know what makes him tick. He lives for the thrill of the chase and the almighty dollar. Like I said, I'm much too old for my age!

As I leave my bedroom, I spot my mom in our quaint, outdated kitchen, trying to pack our lunches and struggling as she does so. "Mom, I'll finish this up," I tell her, grabbing the bread to make my brother's special PBJ and banana sandwich. It's the only one he'll eat.

She flushes with obvious relief. "Thank you, baby girl." I immediately feel guilty that I didn't do this earlier. Mom tries so hard, but she's just not strong enough anymore. Her disease is crippling her slowly, and it's painful to watch. Her body has become her prison. Just another reason I have to try harder for her.

Finishing up packing our sacks, I help mom back to her wrought-iron bed, fluffing the pillows as she reclines. I kiss her cheek, inhaling her unique scent. I know this is where she'll stay for the rest of the day, until we come home. I usher Evan out of the little house in a panic so we won't miss the bus.

I call over my shoulder, "I love you, mom!" *It's just another day in the life of Ella Anderson.*

CHAPTER 3
GRAYSON

Finally, I'm alone in one of the only places where breathing is bearable. Somewhere that's my domain, the ROTC (Reserve Officers Training Corps) room. That's right, Grayson Blackwood is a pro at taking orders and giving them. *The apple doesn't fall far from the tree.* "Yeah, right!" I laugh at myself. Again trying to push away the brutal thoughts of my father and his wayward tactics. Like his father before him, it's all he knows. But it doesn't make it any easier as the bile moves up my throat.

I sit at the table, eagerly leafing through different military colleges; the one that continually catches my eye is The United States Military Academy at West Point. It's located North of New York City on the Hudson River. The application process is long and tedious, and I've been secretly working on mine for the last year. Anticipation and longing stir in my restless soul. Imagining a new beginning away from my current circumstances solidifies my resolve in making my dream a reality.

I sigh, "This is it. My real fuckin' chance of getting away and doing something important with my life."

My father wants me to run the ranch when he retires

to carry on the Blackwood name. He's been relentlessly trying to acclimate me to the whole process, and if I'm honest with myself, that's really not where my interests lie. Somewhere above the Mason Dixon line is where my dream begins.

Being part of ROTC gives me purpose, a meaning that's been cultivating since I first joined. Sergeant Wiley continually guides me on the path to becoming the man I want to be. He saw something in me the first day I walked into his room. I'm grateful for all he does.

Serving my country, doing my duty as an officer in the military, is all I can think about lately. All my hopes and dreams are riding on it, on receiving an appointment to the academy. I've been told you have to be the whole package; smart, a leader, instinctual, they only want the best and... The recruiters have me in their sight! I am at the top of my class. I'm not bragging, but I'm really freaking smart, it comes so easily. Sometimes I choose to act the jokester, 'cause it makes people think they can get one over on me, try to best me.

Playing games is my forte and helps the boredom when you live in a small town. But I don't play games when it comes to applying and getting into West Point. And the best part is, it's a full ride scholarship opportunity. Won't need a cent from the old man. *One less thing he can't hold over my head.*

"I have to be fucking perfect," I mumble to myself. Again relishing in the fact that I can do it. *I have to.* Failure is not an option.

Hearing the classroom door open, I realize my quiet time is over. "Are you coming out to practice or what?" I hear *her* say. Her name is Ella Anderson.

I momentarily say her name over and over in my mind, because it's all I can do without falling hard for this girl. Closing my eyes, I visualize her perfect curves and beautiful dirty blonde hair, with the most electric set of ocean eyes I've ever seen. *Yeah, I've thought about her often.* Ever since Ella and her family moved to town two years ago. The funny thing is, because of all the games I like to play, she thinks I'm nothing. Which is a good thing, because I don't need any distractions from my goals. And this girl is a huge distraction.

She clears her throat again to get my attention. "Hmm. I said, are you coming out to practice or what? We should've started 'bout fifteen minutes ago."

Shit, practice. We are preparing for the National High School Drill Team Championships in Daytona Beach, in two weeks. It's the largest competition we attend and as a unit, we are expected to perform drills with lightweight weapons in military form at a higher level. *This year we will win!*

Ella is annoyed by my nonchalant attitude. Can you blame her? I'm a prick enjoying the annoyance and fire in her eyes when she looks at me that way. It touches a place deep down in my gut and stirs feelings only she can. As I shake out the cobwebs from my brain and focus entirely on her, smirking with confidence, I drawl, "Sure, sweetness, lead the way." Where she leads, I will follow.

Practice begins, and for the remainder of the afternoon it's nothing but drills and routines over and over again. It's a warm and sunny day in the South. Everyone's working up a sweat, and my body's aching in more ways than one. I try to keep my eyes off Ella, but she makes it so damn hard, sashaying that pretty little ass around me even if she is just marching. Her body moves within her tight as fuck jeans, capturing my attention. She catches me looking at her a few times and squirms under my gaze. I shouldn't be acting this way, but why the fuck not? I've lost control and just can't help it. She calls to me like a siren to a sailor.

When we begin to wrap it up, I do the unthinkable. I walk right up to her and ask, "Hey, Ella, do you need a ride home?" as I'm eyeing the trail of sweat between her luscious breasts.

At first, she looks at me as if I'd grown two heads. *Maybe I have!* I laugh out loud and she blushes in that sweet, innocent way that has become my newest game. Then leaning in toward me, she whispers, "Hmmm. Let me think." She taps her index finger on her chin. "Why, yes, I do but...it won't be with you, Grayson."

The way my name slides off her tongue makes me moan. Ella leans back once again, putting her mask back on, and then smirks at me! *That little minx.* She turns around and walks away, just like that. I watch her scrumptious ass move across the parking lot and let out a small growl. I knew in that moment I was done for, it was over for me, I had to have her, no matter the cost!

Ella

As I walk away, my anger begins to boil deep within me. Who in the hell does he think he is? I'm not on the auction block! Jolted back from my momentary lapse of fury, I plaster a fake smile on my face and ask Amy, "Can you believe Grayson Blackwood? He's such an arrogant, little prick."

She laughs at me and smiles that sweet smile only Amy could give and proceeds to tell me, "Oh yes, I believe it. He's so hot! And girl, he's anything but little!" she punctuates. "What's wrong with you anyway? He seems like he's, um, interested in you, Ella, more than just a drill team member."

She raises her eyebrows up and down in a suggestive manner that makes us both give off a round of laughter like we're crazy in the head! After our giggles die down, I look at her seriously.

"Do you really think so? I mean, he doesn't like anyone, ever. He's always just up for a good roll in the hay. Or that's what the rumor is anyway," Ella states as a matter of fact.

Amy looks at me, puzzled. I guess she thinks that's what I need, a good lay in the hay! *Could she be right?* Am I that kind of girl? No. Never have been, never will be. After watching my dad and mom all these years, I realize I want more. I want to be cherished and loved without boundaries. I know it might seem a childish dream to want a hearts and flowers kind of love, but for now I'll hold out. Because I've promised myself it will be different for me. *Besides, Grayson Blackwood is not hearts and flowers!*

Time to change the subject. "So, are you ready to graduate and enlist in the military?" We're ending the school year and Amy will be shipping off to begin her basic training after graduation. I envy her. I'm ready to get started with my life as well.

"Yes and no." She looks almost sad for a moment. I know that look. She's going to miss her family, her friends, and most of all her boyfriend, Brad. Brad's talented with a ball and bat. He's the home run King in the View and in line to get a baseball scholarship to FSU after he graduates next year. *He's Grayson's age.* And because Amy's dream was always to enlist in the military, their lives are moving in different directions.

Amy looks at me again and starts to laugh. I'm so perplexed by this crazy behavior of hers that I inquire, "What now?" She looks over my shoulder and nods.

I turn around cautiously, not sure what to expect, and there he is, in all his beautiful glory: Grayson. He's leaning against his jacked-up, metallic black Ford F250 4X4, staring at us, at me. I can't be sure because of his shades. His golden waves are blowing in the breeze and his perfectly sculpted chest is out on display. He has the biggest smile on his face, not the normal fake smile he usually gives everyone. No, this is a full-fledged smile, and it begins to melt my insides all the way to my core. But I do the only thing I know to do, which I've learned from my father, run!

I turn back to Amy. "Let's go." Giving me a half-hearted smile, Amy gets in and we drive away.

As we pass the Apothecary Drug Store to head over the bridge, I privately scold myself. *I can't get involved with someone like Grayson Blackwood. There's just no way. Definitely not smart. We're too different, come from different sides of the tracks... What game is he trying to play? He can't be serious, not about someone like me... He's a player!*

My thoughts are interrupted as Amy pulls into my drive. I thank her and get out of the car, readying myself for the night. Everything that has to be done before I can get to my own homework and then finally to bed. With a deep breath, I push open the door and announce that I'm home.

CHAPTER 4
GRAYSON

Summer is here and I'm so damn happy! "Woot, woot! Hell yeah," we all cheer as me and my guys are walking out of the school for the last time as juniors. When we come back in the fall, we'll all be seniors. Life is awesome until I reach my car. I see the note hanging on my windshield. I know what it is even before I retrieve it. But I grab it anyway as a feeling of dread washes over me…

Son, as soon as you leave school today, go by and pick up your sister from school. Then you need to be at home as soon as possible to help me finish worming the cows. Can't do it without you. -Dad

My father's been volunteering in the agricultural department at the high school since I was a baby. It's his donation to the community, his time. So it's just normal to get one of his "love" notes on my car. Especially after the confrontation we had this morning. It's his way of keeping control of all things Grayson. And of course he can't act normal and use his phone to text me, he has to leave an old school note. Just like my father, old school to the core. *Fuck me!*

I look over to my friends, who I'd momentarily forgotten about. "Hey guys, I'll have to meet up with you all later tonight. My dad needs me."

Conner, Johnny, Brad, and Pete, better known as Killer, assess me wearily. The looks they give me are some of understanding and some of alarm, because everyone knows my dad's a hardass. But they're good friends, *my posse,* so they all shake it off and nod, sending me on my way to meet up with them later tonight.

Johnny and Connor linger behind as the others pull out of the parking lot. Connor is vague when he mentions an appointment with his dad and a lawyer, and I'm left wondering what the hell that's all about. We fist pump as he gets in his Mustang GT and says he'll meet up with us at the bonfire later tonight.

These two are my best friends. Truthfully, they've been there to pick me up off the ground many a day and helped me to brush it off, move on, hope, and dream. Johnny and Conner are the two people who I've counted on over the years. Never to judge or ask too many questions. *Like the brothers I never had.*

Johnny looks at me with his honest eyes. "Man, I can come help and maybe we can move it along a bit faster. Do you think your dad would mind too much?" I look at him in awe.

"You know how my father can get, man. Are you sure you want to put yourself through that?" I say, laughing a little, but cringing inside.

Johnny just shrugs his massive shoulders and gives a simple, "Yeah." So we get into my truck and begin the journey across town to pick up my little sister, Addie, the sparkle in my darkened existence.

* * *

"Hold on to her, dammit!" my father curses out at me.

We've been at it for hours and we still have five more calves to worm. Not that *dear ole dad* doesn't have help on the ranch to do stuff like this. He does! These heifers are his prize herd, so he won't trust them to anyone. He's won awards for the well-bred stock he's cultivated over the years. Limousin and Hereford cattle crosses make for the perfect mouth-watering combination of meat. Ranchers from all over the United States come to Blackwood Cattle Ranch when looking for champion bulls for breeding. It's been a lucrative business for my family started by my father's father. Hence the hell I'm put through every time these cows have to be taken care of.

Light is beginning to fade into the horizon and we're racing against it to finish the job. That's when all hell breaks loose...The other calves waiting anxiously to be wormed decide that they don't want the attention. They fly up and out over the fence into the adjoining field. I see a flash out of the corner of my eye, as I'm tediously holding on to one calf; Johnny's making a mad dash for the others. My dad is cursing up a storm at this point, and dread filters through my stomach. *I might not get away tonight as I had planned. Shit!*

Then something amazing happens, like the heavens opened up and sent angels down to rescue me. Johnny remarkably herds the escapees back into the corral. I've never seen anything like it, to be honest. He's a magician, an animal whisperer.

Johnny's family owns a much smaller farm not too far down the road. He's always had a way with animals and in this moment, I'm so damn grateful that he's here.

"Way to go, son," my father praises.

A second there I thought he was talking to me, but then my eyes roam to his and they are gazing upon Johnny.

"Sure, no problem, Mr. Blackwood. I'm just glad I was able to grab them when I did!" Johnny laughs, taking in deep, long breaths.

Then my father says the expected, "You could learn a thing or two from this one, Grayson." He sneers at me as he points his thumb toward Johnny.

Years ago that would have rocked me to the core, but I'm numb to it now. I just nod, "Yes, sir."

Honestly, I don't give a shit one way or the other, I'm just glad that it's a save and my night is back on track.

We finish up with the setting of the sun and the humid Florida heat running down our backs. My father thanks Johnny for all his help, sliding a few Jackson's into his palm, and just looks at me. *Same ole, same ole,* I think to myself.

That's my dad's way of things. When the going gets tough, he buys his way through life. That's one of the reasons I have my own monster truck. My father was trying to 'pay me off' for his unbearable treatment. I have everything I could possibly dream of or need...momentarily. Part of the Blackwood package.

After showering, we have a bite to eat of mom's delicious Southern fried chicken and mashed potatoes— that's some good chow. She's trained as a gourmet chef, and her best meals to me always seem to have that Southern flare. Teacher by trade, chef by choice. *I am so lucky at least my stomach is!*

We take our leave and head to the end of the school year party. It's located out in a hay field not too far from our ranch, at Old Man Smart's place. His son, Levi, isn't a good friend of mine, but we aren't strangers either. He's four years older than me and came home for his girlfriend's graduation. His property is situated near Pond Creek, where many of us have enjoyed summer parties over the years.

Johnny and I exit my truck, leaving behind the craziness of the afternoon. We want to get our drink on, and this is just the place to do it. The bonfire's already in full blaze, and the music's blaring loud. *You Can't Take the Honky Tonk out of the Girl* by Brooks & Dunn is currently playing. *Good thing we're in the middle of nowhere,* I think to myself. We help ourselves to a beer from the cooler and begin to walk around and mingle with all our friends. *Yes, I said beer. We are teenagers after all*!

Beer in hand, I walk to the other side of the bonfire, and that's when I see her. Standing there with a red solo cup in her hand, her legs look so long and luscious with those Daisy Dukes and "Mmmm," red cowboy boots! Fist in my mouth, I bite back my groan. She has her hair braided down the sides of her head and the tails fall onto the swell of her pert, supple breasts. I'm drooling at this point. I have to have her. She enthralls, intrigues me, and those eyes. So I do what I do best...put my game face on and approach. *It's game time.*

Coming in from behind, I lean in and whisper into Ella's ear, "Bluebird." Her eyes remind me of the birds on the ranch, vibrant royal blue. The small creatures flitter from post to post, searching for their nest. Always found in pairs.

She's startled at first, but leans into my mouth. I stand stock still, willing my body not to make a sound or a move. However, Mr. Big Shot behind the zipper of my jeans has other plans. Just when I think she's playing along, she turns around and looks at me with those soulful, blue eyes. Giving me a quick bewitching smile and a nod, she turns back toward her group and continues her conversation. *What just happened? She wants to play hard to get...Game on.* I draw myself into the conversation and we all begin to laugh and carry on as if we're long lost friends. *See, two can play this game.* I just want to get her alone and have my way with her.

Ella

The bonfire is blazing a little too hot as I step back a few and stop dead in my tracks. He's here. I was hoping to see him tonight, even if just from a distance. He's wearing a blue shirt that clings tight around his fine physique with those amazing Levi's that always seem to hug all the right places on him, and his famous trademark FSU hat.

My body begins to tingle all over, in all the right places. My belly flutters as an unfamiliar feeling pools in my core. *No, Ella. Too dangerous!* I reprimand myself, knowing that I can't take a chance with anything as magnificent as Grayson Blackwood. But my heart is beating so loudly from its pounding that I can't hear anything else. He disappears behind the massive fire, and for a minute, I have a reprieve. I can't think straight when he's near. He makes me think crazy thoughts. I've kissed a few guys, and yes, I'm a big flirt, but the s-e-x word has never entered my brain! I want to know more. I blush again.

My body starts to tingle again as if on cue, actively seeking, and I know it's him. I feel him coming up behind me, so I just stand casually and ignore it. *I have to ignore it...him!* I think to myself. Feeling his lips brush softly against my neck and up to my ear, I begin to melt.

Just a simple, "Bluebird," is his hello.

But holy hell, it felt anything but simple. Wait. Why did he say bluebird? I'm sure my mind went on hiatus as soon as he touched me, so my body's instincts take over. I turn around slowly and execute the sexiest smile I can muster. It's so damn hard stepping away from his warm, hard body, but I have to, I can't think otherwise. I know that he likes to play games, and I seem to be the next target on his long list, so I give him something to think about. My sexiest smile. Then as casually as I turned around to him, I turn back to my group and pick up the convo as if nothing ever happened. What I didn't expect was for him to saddle up beside me and jump in with both feet. Who knew that Grayson Blackwood was so intuitive, insightful, and actually very smart?

One by one the group breaks up to talk with others, or dance, or do something crazy that goes on at bonfire parties. And we're left just the two of us. I'd laughed so hard when he began to tell the story of the "cow worming" from today. Grayson is hilarious in his own right, but I also see something haunting in those beautiful, brown orbs. A mystery behind his façade, a secret that he is keeping close. I shake my head from all the nonsense going on inside of it.

Grayson looks at me and asks, "Do you want to dance?" extending his hand to me.

That's when I notice that the music has turned soft and sensual. I blush a little, because I really do want to hold his body close to mine. He stares straight into my eyes and lifts his hand further out, beckoning me to take a chance. I reach out and take his hand, immediately feeling all those wonderful, tantalizing tingles, and notice something flash in his eyes I hadn't seen before, fire! And it's burning me up.

GRAYSON

I knew I had her the moment our hands touched. It felt like two magnets being pulled together because of their magnetic properties. That's how it was with Ella; she's the positive to my negative. All night she's been taunting me with her hot and sexy outfit that I just had to have a taste of her.

I begin humming along with the tune *You Can't Hide Beautiful* by Aaron Lines, booming out through the hay field. Swaying her back and forth, I manage to get us even closer than I'd hoped. She seems to be putty in my hands, and I crave it. I've been holding out, trying desperately *not* to have this moment, but here it is. I know she can feel my excitement about our situation pressing hot and hard against her stomach. Still, she makes no move to release the embrace we have wrapped around each other. So I take advantage of our position and lean in to give her my best panty-melting kiss. What I don't expect is how it shakes me to my core.

Grabbing her face in my hands, I tenderly kiss her left eyebrow and make my way to nibble on her earlobe. I give the same attention to the other side of her face, ending with featherlight kisses on her lips. Her sweetness is calling to me, and the uncontrollable urge to take this further overwhelms me. I deepen the dance of our tongues, caressing her lips and tongue softly, yet demanding more. I'm an animal, devouring my prey. Focusing on where we are and knowing how uncomfortable Ella would be, I rein the beast in, severing the kiss, and pull her head toward my chest. Even when the beat of the music picks up, we continue dancing to the tune we've created together. It was a soul-awakening kiss. *Yep, I'm in deep, deep trouble!*

CHAPTER 5
GRAYSON

Summer started off with a bang! That kiss rocked my world and left me yearning for more. *Ella*. She's all I think about. Imagining her body against mine, learning her innermost desires, keeps me in constant pain from not having her. Today's Thursday, and I'm headed to my grandma's house to cut her yard.

Matilda Rose Blackwood is a force to be reckoned with. Don't get her riled up. She's a fierce protector of her family. She grew up on a ranch in Alabama and met my grandfather at the county fair in Lakeview one summer when she had visited her cousins. Theirs was a whirlwind love affair. He swept her off her feet, and before she knew what happened, she was living in Lakeview and was pregnant with my Aunt Polly Jean. Two years later, she had my father, and ten years later, my Aunt Becka was born.

After my grandfather passed years back, she moved from the main house on the ranch into a cottage closer to town and her friends. She said there were too many haunted memories floating around and she was ready for a new beginning. And, it allowed my father to take responsibility of the day-to-day operations that he had been groomed for and had patiently been waiting to slide into. She's the one person in my family I know I can count on no matter what.

I pull up in her front yard and she's waiting in her rocker, sipping her coffee. That woman can drink coffee even when it's a hundred and one degrees outside. "Hey grandma, how's it going?" I ask her.

Leaning forward, watching me walk, she replies, "What's wrong with your back?"

She knows. I can tell. No matter what, she is attuned to my actions, because she's been there, done that, got the ticket and all that jazz. My grandfather was not the nicest person. He killed a man back in the day, for God's sake, had to enlist in the military or go to jail, and she still wouldn't leave him. Being from the archaic, once married always married, till death do us part, is grandma's motto. Thank goodness he passed away before I was born. The things I've heard about him scare the shit out of me.

"Nothing's wrong with me," I reply, knowing I'm not getting off the hook that easily with her. She squints those old, insightful eyes and stares at me as if she's reading my thoughts.

Sighing, she asks, "He's been at it again?" with worry in her voice. She's tried to intervene the same as mom, but somehow it only makes matters worse, not better.

Not answering, I switch topics, "I met someone," knowing this is the sure fire way to get her mind off of my back.

"Really," she answers, drawing out every syllable of the word.

"Yep, I think she's the one for me, maybe my zing," I comment, leaning in to kiss her cheek. My grandma believes that God creates one perfect soul mate for each of us, and once we find them, lightning strikes and you can't deny your destiny. Confirming the possibility I've found the zing to my zang explains how important Ella is to me.

"Well, it's about time, young man, you've been dilly dallying around for so long we've got bets going on how as to if you'd ever have a girlfriend. Between your aunts and sisters, the pot's up to two hundred dollars, and that inside information might help me win it," she smiles, and I begin to ponder what the heck my grandma is talking about.

"Details, sweetie, details!" She continues smiling, and I know laughter will be following soon.

"She's a year younger than me and I know her through ROTC. I've been watching her since she moved here a few years back. I'm thinking of asking her out," I state, uncertainty lacing my voice. I don't want to rush Ella and lose her now that she's actually talking and, um, kissing me.

Grandma sips her coffee and looks toward the ducks swimming in the pond, nodding occasionally at me to continue, and I tell her everything, even about the bonfire kiss that rocked my world. My chest is lighter and breathing seems normal. Little did I know how much I needed my weekly chat with her. Since I can remember, my grandma has sheltered and protected my sisters and me. Her nurturing voice is a balm to my battered soul. Our time together ends when his truck arrives. My father has come to ensure the lawn is done the way he deems it should be done.

"Hi Maw, son," he greets as he exits his truck and slams the door. He looks around, noticing the yard hasn't been touched, and a gleam of hatred is directed at me.

"We've been enjoying the peaceful day, Wood. Grayson was filling me in on his college applications," she says, and I'm grateful once again she knows not to tell him about my new girl. Granny always seems to put fires out, help those in need, and protect her most beloved. Thank the Almighty I'm one of them.

Finally reaching the front porch, he sits in the rocker beside grandma and begins to list the reasons I need to finish here and head back to the ranch, none of which are crucial, but that doesn't matter. He's controlling my actions like the grand puppet master he is. Getting up, I head to the junk house and begin my labor of love for my grandmother, keenly aware that my father is watching my every step and there'll be hell to pay later on.

My father leaves shortly after I start. Thank goodness. Once grandma's yard is done, I head out to meet up with Johnny and Connor for a bite to eat at our favorite hamburger joint in town, Coney Island. It's near the railroad tracks and I get stuck waiting for the noon train to pass before I can savor one of the best burgers in the world, or at least in my world, that is.

We all hang out, drinking ice-cold A&W root beer and talking about going to a party at the beach this weekend. My comments are interrupted when the girl that's been plaguing my every waking hour steps through the door, Ella. Looks like she's got a summer job working for Old Man Cain. Life couldn't be better, since I eat here close to three times a week.

Ella

Walking to work in the dead of summer in Florida's humid heat is not smart. Entering Coney Island, sweat running down my back, I glance at the small table in the front and see Grayson and his friends eating. His head snaps up, and that gorgeous smile I dreamed of last night is drawing me in. Quickly turning away, I scamper to the back room to stick my purse in the borrowed locker and clock in for work. It's not the greatest paying job, but it helps supplement the money needed for my mom's expensive medication.

Returning to the main floor, I run smack dab into a massive chest. I draw in a deep, lustful breath and Grayson's beautiful smell inundates my senses, calming my already wound up body. Hands immediately grab my arms to stabilize the impact, and I look up into those amber eyes. "Where's the fire, sweetheart?" Grayson asks while stroking my arms.

"I'm running behind today and need to help with taking the orders. It's packed in here," I mumble, trying to escape his charms and arms.

Last night, I made a promise to myself that I wouldn't devote any more time to Grayson Blackwood. I have responsibilities that take priority over having a little fling with him. I made a list of pros and cons and well, the cons won. Hands down. He's too good for me, for Christ's sake. He's wealthy, gorgeous, and leaving for college next summer. I have no experience with guys like him. Keeping my mind focused on the future will help me get out of this podunk town and away from the helplessness at home. My dad has started a business he won't talk about. I know we will be moving again soon. It's inevitable.

Looking at Grayson, I whisper, "Look, I know what happened at the bonfire and all, but you and me, well, we can't see each other. And that kiss, it's never gonna happen again. Do you understand? Friends. That's all. I can't kiss you again."

Alarm and hurt register on his handsome face, but I can't worry about him. It's better to severe ties now than be devastated later. Backing away, he shakes his head and walks out of the restaurant without a backwards glance.

What have you done, Ella? I'm distraught, but know

this is for the best. I can't be another notch on his belt. I'm not ready for that yet. I'll never be good enough for him either. Oil and vinegar don't mix, and I'm definitely not sweet as sugar. Pushing all thoughts of Grayson out of my mind, I focus on the task at hand. Taking orders, serving the crowd, this is my life for now.

CHAPTER 6
GRAYSON

The summer seems to drag by as slowly as a slug on a rock. Between ROTC, sports, and the ranch, I didn't have time to pursue the lovely Ella how I planned. Today is the first day of my senior year. I meet up with the guys for breakfast at Tropical Palm, where everyone is talking about football and whether we will make it to the state finals in Tallahassee again this year. Connor and Johnny are at our table when I walk over and sit down.

"Are y'all ready for our senior year and to whoop some fish-head ass this week?" I ask as I motion to the waitress to give her my order.

"Hell yeah! I'm ready," Connor relays, while we all give our order to the waitress.

Johnny doesn't answer as he shakes his head and laughs at the obscene comments we've made. These are the times I'll miss when we all go our separate ways. We've been playing sports together since we were knee high to a grasshopper, and I can't imagine not doing this next year. Since we were five years old, we've played football, basketball, and baseball. Season in and season out. It kept us focused and disciplined.

We finish up breakfast and make it to school before

the first bell rings. That's when my eyes land on her and my palms begin to sweat. She's dressed in a red and black short-sleeved top and painted-on blue jeans. Her hair flows down her shoulders in curls and the light in the room glows around her, causing a halo effect. Mouth-watering beautiful. After her decision to "be friends," I decided that time was on my side. Waiting for her to see me as more, well, that's a challenge I readily accepted. She looks up and catches my stare. So much relayed is in that brief moment as an electrical pulse runs between us, charging both of us, always connected. Yeah, we are so much more than friends.

After class, I catch up with Ella and we walk to her locker. "How was your summer, Bluebird," I ask.

"You know good and darn well how my summer went. I worked! Not all of us can take the time off and enjoy going on vacations or lounging at the beach." *If she only knew.*

She continues, "People depend on me," then slams her locker door and stomps off to her next class.

What the holy hell was that? The little imp unloaded her mind on me, and I was completely unprepared with a comeback as I watched her grab her books and head to her next class. No worries, I'll talk to her after school.

After practice, I make a beeline to Ella. She's talking to Sarah about the movie they plan to see this weekend, Harry Potter and the Prisoner of Azkaban. Never would have thought she would be into those movies too. It's one of my all-time favorite book series.

Jo used to read them to us at night.

"Ella, you got a minute? I need to talk to you about earlier," I interrupt their conversation and grab her arm. She looks stunned and cautiously follows my lead. Once we are out of everyone's hearing, I ask her why she was so short this morning.

Exhaling a long breath, she says, "Sorry, Grayson. I didn't mean to come across so harsh. It's been a rough few weeks. My mom's health is getting worse and it hurts watching her in so much pain, and my dad's being such a friggin' jerk about it. Why the hell can't he show her a little compassion? She's dying, you know, d-y-i-n-g."

I glimpse the tears forming in her eyes and pull her close to me, knowing she needs a hug. I've never met her mom, but I know it would destroy me if something happened to mine.

"You've had a rough time, haven't you, Bluebird?" All of sudden it comes to me. My new game plan for Ella. "I've got a proposition for you. How 'bout you and me try being friends and just hang out together and see where this," I point my finger between her and me, "goes. What do you say, Ella? Deal?" I hold my breath, waiting for her answer.

I watch her face as she considers my proposition. She's unsure about what I've asked. I wonder if that's because she cares for me. After what seems like hours but is only a few seconds, she starts nodding her head up and down. That's all the answer I need as I close my arms around her, letting her take what she needs from me. I'll be her friend, for now.

Ella

It's Christmas time. One of the best times of the year. Today, I'm at home with my mom and Evan, decorating our tree. It reminds me a little of Charlie Brown's tree, small but full of love. The smell of chocolate chip cookies baking fills the air as Bing Crosby sings *We wish You a Merry Christmas* on the radio. We all chime in and sing along as we plug in the lights to the tree. *I will miss moments like these when she's gone.* Plastering a huge smile on my face, I begin singing again and grab the next ornament to hang.

Since the beginning of school, so much has happened. I can't stop thinking about the past few months with Grayson. He's been relentlessly pursuing me. He won't let me go. Everywhere I turn, he's there. If I'm at work, he shows up, orders a drink, and sits quietly watching me take orders and serve food. When we're at drill practice, he sneaks quick, sexy as hell winks at me.

Sarah and I went to the movies last weekend. When we were exiting the theatre, there he was, waiting to drive me home. It's like he can't help himself. The funny thing is, I like it. No, I crave his attention. My anticipation of what he'll do next keeps me on my toes.

We've spent many afternoons after drill practice sitting on the bed of his jacked-up truck at the school, talking about so many things. My future, his future, where we see ourselves in five years, ten years. The more I get to know the real Grayson Blackwood, the more I approve. He's not at all how I perceived him to be, or like the raunchy rumors going around school for that matter.

I've found out that Grayson has a true fondness for all his sisters, even with the age difference. They are much older than him and Addie. He's told me stories about each one of them. I'm drawn into all his versions of them and am becoming more and more impressed with him.

One afternoon while reminiscing about his family, he mentioned, gazing up toward the horizon, "The leash has to be taken off. It's not gonna happen till I can break away from him. It's a pattern, Bluebird. They all got out of here, and that's what I plan to do too."

When I questioned him more about his statement, he just leaned in, gave me a peck on the cheek, and said, "No worries, Bluebird. I'm gonna do something really important and it doesn't involve staying in this town."

I let it go, because at that point, thinking about the possibility of him leaving was unbearable for my heart. Although these feelings I've cultivated for him are getting stronger and stronger. I'll be devastated when he's no longer here. My reaction is inescapable.

Winter approached with a cold spell or two, quite normal for this Florida coastal town. With the season, it also brought my seventeenth birthday. Grayson surprised me with an exquisitely crafted pink heart charm as my gift, which he delivered personally during our lunch break in the school cafeteria. I was completely shocked as he walked toward me, holding my present in one hand and a lit pink cupcake in the other. He began singing, "Happy Birthday to you…" and before I realized it, the whole cafeteria filled of my peers was singing along with him like the chorus at a recital. A humbling moment, for sure. I still wasn't sure what the pink charm was for, but I accepted it because it was from him.

Then one day before holiday break, Grayson gave me an elegant platinum charm bracelet with an army charm hanging off it, and that's when the pink heart charm clicked.

"Oh, wow…just wow, Grayson. This is an amazing gift." My eyes pooled with unshed tears from the tenderness of his gift.

The enormity of his gesture cracked the surface around my heart! It's the most precious present anyone has ever given me. I had nothing to give him in return, except my friendship along with a hug and a kiss on the cheek.

"I didn't expect something in return, Bluebird. Just wanted to see that sparkle in your gorgeous eyes and know that I put it there," he motioned to my smiling face and then laid his hand over his heart. "I wanted you to have something from me. 'Tis the season of giving and kissing and mistletoe, right?" We both burst into laughter at his silly but heartfelt words.

Grayson's vocabulary and presentation will be the death of me. He keeps tearing down the walls I've built. Walls to protect my heart. And for now, we continue on, without being 'more than friends'. He mutes my insecurities and soothes my soul. I'm growing more dependent upon his charming heart.

GRAYSON

My father's been acting strange the past few months. I can't quite put my finger on it. He hasn't been watching my every step for a mistake. No notes left on my truck at school. No snide remarks. I've even approached him about attending West Point again, and he didn't overreact or comment. When I questioned mom, she didn't help at all, saying she had noticed the lack of interaction between us.

I didn't make curfew last Saturday night, because I was helping Johnny fix his flat tire and totally lost track of time. When I arrived home, I was expecting the worst, and what greeted me set uneasiness to linger.

"Grayson, where have you been, son?" my mom started the interrogation, only to be interrupted by father.

"You're late," he stated as he got up from his recliner in the family room. I braced myself for impact.

I stuttered and began rapidly explaining what happened, only for him to continue down the hallway without acknowledging my words. Stunned that he didn't attack me, I looked to my mom for answers. She shrugged and nodded her head left to right, biting her bottom lip with worry.

"He's been tired lately, son," she commented as she hugged me and followed him to bed. *Huh? Weird.* But, I'm not allowing him into my psyche to play mental games. His change will have to be more than that for me to forgive or forget a lifetime of hurt.

As puzzling as my father's actions have been over the last few months, they've also allowed me freedom from the ranch. I've spent as much time as I can with Ella. Since we are only friends, we normally hang out with our group of friends. Just friends. It works for now, but I'm preparing her for more. She's not ready to accept it yet. One day she'll be all mine.

CHAPTER 7
GRAYSON

It's Valentine's Day and I found Ella a bluebird charm. We are at the bowling alley when I give it to her. She just finished her turn and sits back down.

"Hold out your hands, Ella. Close your eyes, and you will get a big surprise!" I laugh at her beautiful face and scrunched-up nose, so damn cute. She's hesitant at first, eyeing me skeptically.

"What are you up to, Mr. Blackwood?"

She closes her eyes and follows my instructions. She opens her eyes and her gaze lands on the palm of her hand, where a dainty bluebird charm lies. Shock registers on her face and then glee.

She continually asks me why I call her Bluebird, and my reply is always the same, "You're my Bluebird, Ella," shrugging my shoulders like it's no big deal. I think she likes her special name. One day, I'll explain it to her, but we aren't there...yet.

Why Bluebird? I fondly remember a time when I was around ten years old. Mom's really crafty being the teacher that she is. We decided to make bluebird boxes for all the ones we had on the ranch.

"Come on, Grayson. It'll be loads of fun. Addie

can even help us." Mom giggled as we made our way outside to the barn. Moments like these I'll cherish forever, they're my memories that no one can take away.

It was a hot summer day on our ranch. We set out constructing, cutting boards, hammering nails, and then painting our initials on the front of each box. Mom sang "Whistle while you work..." from Snow White, and Addie jumbled some of the words as she tried to sing along, shaking her three-year-old baby bootie back and forth. It was a perfect day.

Later on in the evening after we all showered and got ready for dinner, Mom came looking for me. I'm in my room, staring out the window at one of our newly built bluebird boxes. The delicate box is perched right outside my window, waiting for visitors. We put this one in this spot, so I could see it every day.

"Grayson, it's time for dinner, son." Mom leaned against the door, watching me. "What are you up to?"

"Watching the box," I tell her. "I can't wait for the birds to come."

Mom moved over to where I was sitting on the floor and sat down beside me. "Oh, I see. Well, let me tell you a little story then.

"Once upon a time there was a little boy bluebird, who loved his family very much. The little bluebird wasn't old enough to have his own family yet, so his family protected him, even when he didn't know it. One day, a new little bluebird came to town, fluttering *around their nest. She too had a family, and the little boy bluebird was very interested in her. The two little bluebirds became instant friends. Going on adventures, playing together, and having fun. They even learned how to fly further away from their nests...together. One day, a strong storm came through, huffing and puffing all the nests in the trees. The little boy bluebird was tossed out of the nest and carried on the wind far away. Thought to be lost forever. When the storm subsided, the little boy bluebird saw his friend was there too. Both being thrown away from home by the storm, they were scared, but they had each other. As the weeks passed and their search for home continued, they learned to hunt for food. And before they knew it, they were building a nest together in a sturdy box up against a tree. Never leaving the other or straying too far away. Because bluebirds mate for life."*

The story my mom told me reminds me of Ella. It's the reason why I call her Bluebird.

* * *

Before long, we are all ready to escape the everyday life of school and practice. Thank god for spring break! Baseball season is in full swing, and we're going to State. *Yeah! That's right, we're that good!* But right now, it's time for a hiatus from the craziness of life. Our posse is heading to the beach for the week. Conner's parents own a house on the Gulf, and for the next week, it's fishing, beer, and relaxing with my friends.

On my way out of town, I stop by to see Ella. She's getting ready for work. She has so many responsibilities and obligations; thinking about it creates a huge lump in my throat. I do too, but mine involves controlling all things Grayson. Not like Ella, trying to make ends meet.

Opening the door, Ella greets me with her brilliant smile. "Hey, Grayson! Let's talk outside. My mom's taking a nap and I don't want to wake her up," she mutters, pushing me through the door and closing it softly.

"You working all week, Bluebird?"

She sighs, "Yes. Mr. Cain has me on the schedule every day with school being out. It's good though, we really need the money."

"Well, shit! I wanted to see if you could come to the beach with me. Conner's family has a house down there and we're going to do some fishing and other stuff."

I'm struck by how dumb that sounds once the words leave my mouth. This girl is working to help her family. Ella doesn't need me to add to her hardships. I rethink and start over.

"Sorry, I just want to spend a little more time with you, is all. I understand duty."

I gaze into her pools of blue, while my hands seize her waist, pulling her in for a hug. Her smell intoxicates me, sending ripples of desire over my shoulders, down my spine straight to my groin. *Fuck, I want this girl.*

Ella looks into my eyes, and I see something sparkle, desire. Leaning in, I sneak a peck on her neck, moving up to her ear, leaving soft wet kisses in my wake. Ella stiffens, and I hear her breath catch. I play a little more with her neck and feel her relaxing in my hold. Moving to the corners of her lips, I watch her reaction: flushed cheeks and parted mouth. Dragging my teeth across her bottom lip, slowly, methodically pouring the attraction, I feel for Ella into my every touch, finally capturing her lips with mine as I impart my need for her.

Breathlessly, she jerks away and our moment has passed. "That was ... it was ... what was that for, Grayson?" Ella is flustered and I like it.

Drawing Ella's hands into mine, I bring them to my mouth, kissing each knuckle carefully while keeping my eyes on hers.

"I'll miss you this week, Bluebird."

Leaving her on the porch at her house is hard for me. It's going to be rough not seeing her for the week, and my body aches to claim her. Surprise doesn't even cut the reception she gave me. Baby steps. She allowed me to kiss her again, and it was overwhelming. Timing is everything. She'll be mine soon enough. I head out down to the beach to go chill with the guys.

Pulling up to Conner's beach house, I notice there are a lot more cars than I expected. I guess the party started without me. As I put my truck in park and glance at the cottage, Conner comes around the corner to greet me.

"Are you ready to par-tay?" he asks in a sing-song voice that cracks me the hell up! "Come on, Grayson. Let's do this!" Conner grabs the front of my 4X4, hopping up onto the bumper, jumping up and down like a madman. "Welcome to the par-tay!" *He's not right.*

I shake my head at my insane friend. I take a deep breath and grab my bag as I meander out of my truck and set out for a week full of fun.

Later, my feet sink down into the coarse sand prickling my toes as I walk down to the water. I grab another beer from the red cooler situated between our setup and recline back into my lounge chair. The blazing sun is reflecting off the water, and my eyes squint behind my Ray-Bans. A salty breeze tickles my skin. People are splashing in the bay, boats are whizzing by, and a calm settles over me. As much as I'm ready to leave, this is home.

Conner is spread out on his chair along with Johnny, Pete, and Brad. I'm surrounded by my friends.

"I was thinking about prom," Conner starts. "We need a hummer limo…"

CHAPTER 8

Ella

"Ella. Ella, can you please come here for a minute?" mom calls out to me from the other room.

I impatiently move through the narrow hallway to the living room to find mom. Instantly, I feel awful for not wanting to talk, even though I've got a mountain of homework left to do for finals. Mom is getting worse every day, and I should want to spend every moment I can with her. It's just that sometimes I long to be a normal teenager.

My mom is lying on the couch with a book in her trembling hands. I notice the terse look of pain on her face and wince. "Ah, there you are, my beautiful girl," mom sighs.

As I watch her tenuous face, I walk over to sit down beside her and put her feet on my lap. "What's up, my favorite mother in the universe?" I try for a joke in such a tense moment.

Mom lays the book across her chest and takes in a deep, painful breath. "I just want to talk to you about prom."

"Not again, mom! We've already been through this conversation and I told you there isn't any way for me to go this year!" I snap in a miffed voice.

F. G. ADAMS

I just can't do this again. My mom keeps telling me
that I need to go, I have to go, but I just don't see how.
Money is tight. The job I have at the Coney Island is
helping a little, but not enough to splurge on something
as wonderful as prom. I internally sigh and look back at
my mom. That's when I see tears in her eyes, and I'm
done for.

"Oh, no, mom. Please don't cry. I'm so sorry I
snapped at you."

I snuggle up to her, wrapping my arms around her,
holding her in the tightest embrace she can handle in her
fragile state. Grabbing the box of tissues from the
coffee table, I wipe her tears away and listen to what I
know will be my undoing.

"Ella, baby. You have to go, for me. This may be
the last prom I can experience with you. You
understand?" she calmly pleads.

My mom is such an attractive woman, even in her
sickly circumstance. I've always thought she had a
Marilyn Monroe type bombshell appearance with an
angel's heart of gold. Utterly striking. Until lately; the
sickness is smothering out all the outer beauty that is my
mom. But her inner strength, determination, and love
are something to marvel at. I can't help but admire her.
She's always told me the eyes are the windows to the
soul. In this moment as I gaze deeply into my mom's, I
see the pleading and her unconditional love she has for
me. With that, I concede.

"You win, mom. I'll do it," I reply. "I just don't

know where I'm going to get a dress and shoes...it's impossible. You know how tight money is right now. We can barely afford your medications."

My mom's face transforms into the most beautiful smile that even reaches her big baby blues. *I haven't seen this in a long while. Gorgeous!*

"Well, I have that covered for you, baby girl." Mom continues, "I've already talked with Amy. She keeps up with me, you know, even though she's away in the army. And you know she went last year to prom. She has the perfect dress for you to use, shoes and all!"

I blush all over, thinking about the sexy black, sequined dress she's talking about. I saw Amy's pictures last year and fell in love with the dress immediately. It hugs every curve and goes to the floor, but has a slit up both sides, stopping at mid-thigh. The strapless top v's on the front and bottom which gives a barely there look. The nude body holds the sequins, giving the illusion of wearing only a top attached with a skirt. It's utterly gorgeous and very sexy. As if my mom knows my inner dialogue, she gets my attention.

"It's a really beautiful dress, Ella. It will look even better on you," she promises.

Relenting, I hug her tightly. "Thank you, mom. Will you do my hair? You know how to make me look my best. I, uh, mean if you feel like it?" As she nods yes, my mind wonders about what Grayson will look like in a tux, because I've got to go to prom with my best friend. Yeah, right, best friends. He's become so much more, and then there's the good-bye kiss we shared before he left for the beach. I've been dreaming about it for weeks. The anticipation of sharing another one with Grayson is constantly on my mind, combined with what could happen if I let myself go.

GRAYSON

Pulling up to the small house in a not so great part of town, my heart begins to pound out of my chest. I'm nervous as shit! Knowing that Ella lives here still makes my heart ache every time I see it. I just want to take her away from all of this and protect her, keep her safe, and give her the world.

On the ride over to Ella's, Amy kept staring at me, and I got the feeling she wanted to say something. After a few awkward minutes, I finally ask her, "What's up?"

"I'm concerned about Ella's emotional attachment to you, Grayson," Amy tells me. "And your physical attraction to her really worries me," she admits.

"I assure you, Amy, we are only friends." I give her my best smile, but I know she can tell I feel differently. It's written all over my face.

Amy gets the craziest look on her face and says, "I know who you are, Grayson Blackwood. I'm warning you now, DO NOT break Ella. Ella is new to relationships and naïve at best. I don't want to be picking up all the missing pieces when you leave her."

Not gonna happen. "Don't get twisted up about this, Amy. I promise you, hurting Ella is the furthest thing from my mind."

Being honest with myself, it is. I want Ella so bad, nothing else matters.

"That's the problem, Grayson." Amy glances at me once more as the car stops.

Just friends, remember. I struggle with my inner voice, because my heart is saying something very different. Ever since we made our pact, I've been trying so hard to keep it, but she is just so perfect, so right for me. I want her to see the real me.

As we all file out of the stretch Hummer limo, thanks to the wonderful wisdom of our best bud, Conner, I notice a woman sitting in a rocker on the front porch. Instantly, I know it has to be Ella's mom. I've never had a chance to meet her. She's a beautiful woman. Even though sickness and death seem to dominate her on the outside, there is a glow about her, a beauty that's not just skin deep. Much like the girl I've gotten to know pretty well over this past year. The dark circles around her eyes and sunken cheeks are a dead giveaway for the hideous disease that is plaguing her body.

She leans up a bit from the rocker and smiles, saying, "Hello."

I fall hook, line, and sinker for the beautiful aura that surrounds Ella's mom. Feeling all warm and fuzzy on the inside just from her simple 'hello'. I lean toward her

F. G. ADAMS

with my hand out and shake her hand gently.

"Hello, Mrs. Anderson. I'm Grayson Blackwood. Nice to finally meet you in person."

She gently takes my hand in hers, putting her other hand on top.

"Very nice to meet you, Grayson Blackwood."

Mrs. Anderson smiles and winks at me genuinely. Just then the worn, brick red front door opens. And out steps the most beautiful living creature I've ever seen. *Ella.*

I watch Ella walk gracefully to her mom and kiss her on the cheek. They share a glance toward me, as well as a secret smile that only a mother and daughter can. I'm speechless and a lump forms in my throat.

I'm so fucking glad Conner came up with the idea of everybody going to prom together. All of us are close friends, well except for Amy and Brad. The fact that we invited Brad ensured me that Amy would get Ella to come along with us. Amy's been deployed on a tour of duty in Germany for the last nine months and was due her leave. Talk about timing. It was perfect that she came home to go to prom with Brad. I knew that would be the only way we could go together, without going together. The plan was perfect. If all goes well, Ella will become mine tonight. If she'll play along; and if not, then I'll have to persuade her otherwise.

Turning away from her mother, Ella whispers, "See ya later, mom."

"Bye, baby girl. Y'all be careful now. Have lots of

fun. Don't do anything I wouldn't do!" Ella's mom jokingly states. "Make sure to watch out for each other. Oh, and Grayson...you take good care of my baby," she adds, waving.

I can't believe that just happened. Did her mom just tell me to behave, or was she giving me permission? I shake the cobwebs from my brain on obvious overload and respond, "Yes, ma'am. You have nothing to worry about," I announce for the whole world to hear.

Did I really mean that though? Nope, if I can get Ella alone for one minute...

My thoughts are interrupted by a few hushed giggles, and then we all make our way to the limo. Taking a good look at the goddess in front of me, I am speechless yet again. That black dress she has on is wreaking havoc on all my senses, and Mr. Big Shot is making an appearance. The back is low cut with sequins sparkling all around the edge, sitting just above her delectable ass. It hugs every curve, every beautiful place on her body. *Man, what I'd give to take my tongue and lick from top to bottom. Damn, I'm so jealous of her dress.* Her dirty blonde hair is piled high up on her head with gentle curls falling around her face, which makes her look almost angelic. But the view of her neck makes me want to take a bite. *Down, boy! Shit, I'm horny!*

I'd known for a while now that I was falling hard for this girl. She has the power to bring me to my knees with just a look.

CHAPTER 9

Ella

Cinderella at the ball. This night is pure and simply magical! I can't believe I'm actually here with my friends and...Grayson. The way he keeps looking at me, like he wants to devour me—*giggle*—I might just break my resolve. He's been so patient with me all year, and we've actually gotten to know each other pretty well. He makes me feel so comfortable when he's near, gives me a sense of peace and home. How all that happened, I'm not sure. 'One day at a time,' he likes to say. The sexual tension between us has been building every day, every moment we're together. Soon, the dam will burst and I'll be lost to everything Grayson. But one thing's for sure, Grayson wormed his way into my heart, I'll never be the same.

The Hilton ballroom is filled with opulence, beautiful star- and moon-shaped lights strung up along the walls and ceiling covering the entire space. The tables are decorated elegantly with dark red table clothes, candles floating in a centerpiece of flowers, sand, and rocks. The DJ is playing *Burn* by Usher. Every single detail screams glamor, beauty, and romance.

"Penny for your thoughts, Bluebird," Grayson interrupts my ongoing inner monologue.

My breath catches in my throat at the sight of him. Grayson Blackwood is a magnificently created individual. The black tux he's wearing is cut to form fit every muscle along his well-defined structure. The silver tie is loosened, and the button undone just beneath. His soft blonde curls on the top of his head wave at me, filling me with a longing to reach out and touch. *Ugh, get it together, Ella,* I chastise my wayward thoughts.

"Well, I was just sitting here in this magical room full of sparkling lights and wondering when I'm gonna take advantage and dance. I really need to, since we've already been here for an hour, but I just haven't yet," *Breathe.* I'm rambling. One of the things he causes to happen when he's around me.

Grayson reaches out his hand to me and I take it. Drawn like a moth to a flame, it can't be helped. He leads me out onto the dance floor and circles his big arms around me. A sense of peace washes over me. It's like there's no one else in the room but us.

GRAYSON

This is the greatest feeling in the world. As we're slow dancing on the dance floor, with my arms wrapped tightly around Ella's alluring body, I know I want more with her. She is the light to my darkness.

Nothing else matters right now. Not my father, not graduation, not even leaving to go off to West Point. It's like a continuous dream of happiness, one I don't want to wake up from.

"Are you enjoying yourself as much as I am, Bluebird?" I ask in hopes she won't deny these feelings we have for each other another minute.

I look down into her exquisite blue eyes and am lost. Drowning in a swirling sea of boundless blue. Her breath hitches and tangibly, her resolve slowly weakens. So, being the man I am, I lean in close to seal the deal. Ever so gently I place featherlight kisses on both sides of her mouth, watching her eyes while the dance continues.

"You're so beautiful, Ella," saying her name on my lips caresses my inner animal in just the right way.

Before realizing what's happening, Ella grabs hold of my face with both hands and crushes her lips to mine. *Ecstasy!* Our tongues move in sync, tasting, affirming, loving. I have to stop this before it goes too far with an audience, even though I think, *Fuck, who cares what others may think*. For Ella though, I have to. Softly, my lips retreat from her face to her neck and I breathe her in. Both our hearts are beating so loudly as we inhale deep, languid breaths.

"Would you like to go for a walk, Bluebird? Maybe down on the beach?" I ask, hoping she won't say no.

I patiently wait for an answer, then she responds,

"Yes, let's get out of here."

When her answer finally registers in my lust-filled brain, I take action, not giving Ella time to change her mind. Taking her hand, I drag her to the veranda. Outside, the moon is shining brightly against a backdrop of black water, white waves, and the sounds only the Gulf of Mexico can give. I hug her close to my body and we stand soaking in the moonlit night, taking in the surrounding beauty. My eyes drift to hers, and she's watching me intently. I grab one more quick, intense kiss and a towel from a basket before we make our way down the path to where the ocean meets the sand.

We walk hand in hand for a while, just bathing in the moonlight, until I see a spot a little far out, so no one will see us. I lay out the huge hotel towel on the sand, thanking myself for thinking of it. Ella and I sit side by side, listening to the ocean breeze, the waves, and the peaceful, serene night.

"Thank you," she gestures to the towel beneath us. "I couldn't or wouldn't have thought so quickly," she giggles.

There it is, the beautiful sound that has my whole body standing at attention. I angle myself so that my lips touch her creamy, delicate shoulder, placing several soft kisses as I go.

"You're welcome, Ella. Anything for you."

The moment heats up when she peeks up at me through long, luscious lashes. It's a look that says *I want you, I need you.* In a flash, my blood boils, and

Mr. Big Shot wants to come out and play. But I've come to realize this with Ella is so much more than a game.

We have an intense connection. Our bodies mingle and intertwine as I gently lay her back. I cover her completely with mine as her legs fall open, letting me in, an invitation that she wants me as much as I want her.

Needing this moment to last forever, I begin to touch, feel, taste every part of her body that isn't covered with my lips and hands. I pant in and out, fire licking down my back. Ella moans and I'm lost. As my hand slides up her thigh, I bite back a growl. *Shit! What are you doing, Grayson? This isn't the place to love this girl. She deserves better. Remember what Amy said.*

Regaining some sense of nobility, I ask, "Would you like to go back to my room with me, Ella?"

Still gasping for air, she looks at me with those heart-warming baby blues and nods her head. Without giving her a chance to change her mind, I lift her up into my arms, carrying her back to the hotel, to my bed, forever in my heart.

Ella

Holy Hell! What am I doing? While I'm being

carried back to the hotel—*yes, I said carried*—questions begin to assault my lust-filled brain. I know I want to be with Grayson so bad it hurts. He's like an addiction and I'm dying for my next fix. *Can this really be true? Is this just another game? Can I really do this? Give him a piece of me that no one has ever touched?*

I squelch all those thoughts the moment he sets me down beside the elevator to push the button. Grayson looks at me with those beautiful amber eyes and I'm lost again. *This is right, this moment, him...me...*

As the elevator opens, he ushers me in, and the door begins to close. At once, he gently shoves me up against the elevator wall, caging me in.

"I'd give anything to know what you're thinking right now, Bluebird," he says in that raspy, masculine voice I've grown to adore. The same voice that makes me weak in the knees and tingly in all the right places.

Talking isn't what I want at the moment though, so I do the next best thing. I kiss him. Our kisses turn from warm to fierce in a matter of a few seconds. Not realizing the door has opened on our floor, we both turn our heads when we hear a throat clear.

"Well, well, well, what do we have here?" an entertained Conner asks.

Seeing the shit-eating grin that Conner displays so often, I instantly begin to blush. We're caught; our moment is over. Without saying a word, Grayson leads me out of the elevator. As we pass by Conner, the two exchange a look and nod their heads. *Not sure what that's all about? Man code?*

Grayson has his hands all over me, so forgetting all about the unspoken communication is unavoidable. He backs me into the door of his room and proceeds to pass the keycard through the designated spot.

As the lock clicks softly, the door moves to open, and I'm lifted off my feet as Grayson carries me into the room. My senses are bombarded with a multitude of things. The lights are off, but there's a gentle glow to the room. Candles are lit all around on every sturdy surface. The sensual sounds of music play softly in the background. Rose petals are all over the floor, as well as the massive king sized bed that stands tall in the middle of the room. The sweet smell of the flowers is a balm to my otherwise chaotic body. I can't believe what I'm seeing.

As if noticing my shift, Grayson replies, "Do you like it, sweetheart?" as he places me gently down on my feet.

I'm in shock as I nod my head. *He did all of this for me?*

"I wanted to give you a night to remember. Something you could keep with you even when I'm far away," he says. "I was hoping for this anyway," he smiles sheepishly. I see his dimples in the dimly lit room.

"It's all magical, Grayson. I just don't know what to say." I finally get out of my suddenly parched throat.

"You don't have to say anything, Ella. Just let me

love you. Even if it's just for this one special night," he whispers. "Let me show you how much you're wanted and what you do to me."

Time stands still as he reaches for me, pulling me into his heavenly embrace.

CHAPTER 10
GRAYSON

Holding Ella in my arms so close is a moment forever etched in my memory. Realizing she's my zing comforts my restless soul. *She's mine.* Holding her gaze while Alicia Keys sings in the background "*I keep on falling in and out of love...*" we begin to dance the ancient movements of old. Bodies melding into one. She is soft and pliable in my arms.

Her nipples pebble through the thin silkiness of her dress, caressing my chest as my breath begins shallow pants. Not wanting this moment to end, my hands reach for her, pulling her forward, capturing her mouth. Our tongues duel for dominance, each of us fighting for air. The restlessness in my soul screams to be sated, yet I know she needs me to move slowly.

Looking into her eyes, I see the apprehension, which allows me to calm my body and focus on her. She needs this as much as I do, and knowing that helps. This isn't my first rodeo, and knowing that she is innocent brings out the alpha in me. Capturing her lips in one more aggressive move, I begin peeling off her dress. Starting with the zipper at the back, moving it down slowly as to not scare the beautiful creature standing before me. The dress pools at her feet, leaving her in a lacy black bra with a sinful matching thong and stilettos. The garments only accentuate the beauty that is Ella. Long, supple legs and curves capture my view. Clinging to my arms, she stands there in her most beautiful glory, waiting for what comes next.

"Damn Ella, you are perfect," I compliment during my assault on her body. "I can't get enough, can't touch enough of you. I need you so much."

We begin dancing, touching, feeling, loving every inch of our bodies. Mine, hers. I'm not sure where she begins or I end. She grabs my shirt and pulls it from my pants. One by one the buttons are released and her hands touch my flesh. Fumbling, she reaches for my pants and releases the zipper, brushing her hand against my now thick, hard shaft. Her movements are erratic as she drops my pants and boxers to the floor. Glancing up from her bent position, she hesitantly reaches for my cock.

"Fuck, Ella, what are you doing?" I whisper as she caresses my erection. She licks her bottom lip, and my moan fills the room. When she looks up to me for direction, I put my hand over hers, showing her what feels best. We continue to pump my dick, squeezing firmly when she leans forward and boldly licks the pre-cum from the tip. My body's in shock when she takes me into her mouth and her head bobs up and down as she gives me pleasure. She's awkward at first before she settles into a rhythm of her own. Soon, my hips begin to move, and I know this will end before it begins if I don't stop her. Not being able to take much more, I pull her up to me and crash my mouth to hers.

Standing her up, I remove her bra and begin my assault. My lips capture her neck like a thirsty man in need of a drink. Her dusty rose nipples call for me and my tongue lavishes one, while my fingers pinch and pull the other. Ella's soft moan penetrates the quietness. When her nipple is standing painfully erect, I move to the other side, giving it the same time and attention. Her hips begin moving, wanting more.

In the next moment, we're standing before each other in a most compromising position. Both of us naked. My gaze travels over her body as my hands skim over her waist, causing her flesh to pucker as I cup her pert nipples. All I can think about is taking her, claiming her as my own, as my mouth does the tango on her body. I lift her in my arms and carry her to the bed.

"I need you." It's my promise to her. Always.

Laying her down on our bed for the night, I kiss her belly button, moving downward, licking, tasting, savoring. Caught in the dance as old as time itself, I move down her body, kissing my way toward her honey. Alarmed, she begins to close her legs, holding my shoulders.

"No!" she shrieks. Crawling back up her body, I soothingly kiss her fears away and before long, she's moaning my name again. *I have to get my cock in her soon!* I'm about to explode without even being inside of her.

Ella

My body's on fire and it's almost bordering on pain. What's happening to me? Everywhere Grayson touches me ignites unknown feelings of immense pleasure, something I've never experienced before. My body is wanting, pleading for a release I never believed possible.

Doubts begin to enter my fog-filled brain. *If we are intimate, will he still be my friend? What will happen when he leaves for college?* All these thoughts rapidly fade away as he tenderly caresses my clit. Then a finger enters where no one has ever been before. Scissoring and pumping rapidly. Oh god, what's happening to me? Then I feel his tongue caressing my clit at the same time. I'm soaring. My body no longer belongs to me. It's his. Pleasure crawls up my spine, through my body, in a massive feeling of bliss. My stomach tightens and I begin to fall into mind-blowing pleasure.

"GRAYSON!" explodes from me as spasms encompass my body.

GRAYSON

When she screams my name, the small amount of

control I possess snaps. I can no longer wait to make her mine. Grabbing a condom off the nightstand, I rip it open and slide it on. Slowly maneuvering myself on top of Ella, I begin grinding my cock against her wet and slippery slit. Lubricating the condom with her cum, my dick begins probing her opening. Using my hand to guide my throbbing erection inside, I slide in and out in small short thrusts until I'm met with resistance. Her body tenses and I stop to look into her passion-filled eyes. My hands find their way to loop around her shoulders to hold her in place, and I kiss her, hoping it relays my feelings for her.

"You're mine now, Ella. You'll always be only mine," I promise as my hips draw back and push forward through her virginity. Her scream of pain fills my ears, sealing us together.

Not moving a muscle, I count to ten, giving her time to adjust to my invasion. Our panting breaths mingle and I kiss her closed eyes one at a time, nibbling and licking down her throat, behind her ear to the soft spot that makes her wanton. Building the passion back that was lost from the pain, I slip my fingers between our bodies and stroke her clit. Her hips begin to move and I slowly withdraw my throbbing cock almost all the way to only drive back into her tight, hot pussy. Her hips meet mine as our rhythm is found.

Her moans are driving me wild. My body is on a precipice of release and I need Ella with me. Finding her nipples again, I suck, licking and biting, while my fingers stroke her clit faster and our pace picks up speed. She's on the edge when I feel her body begin to tremble and once again, she's screaming my name while she milks my cock, pulling me into my orgasm with her. When I begin to collapse, my arms losing strength from the soul shattering moment we've shared, I roll us onto our sides so we're facing each other, slipping from her body at the same time. Her eyes are closed and a satisfied grin is on her lovely face.

Moments later, I gather my strength and head to the bathroom to dispose of the condom. I return with a warm washcloth and gently clean my girl. She's shy at first, but I won't allow her to turn away from me. We curl up together, arms and legs laced around each other. Ella's head is perched on my hammering chest.

"Thank you, Grayson."

"For what, Bluebird? It's me who should be thanking you. What you just gave to me," I pause, "changed my life forever."

Ella snuggles back down and drifts off to sleep. I watch her for a while. *I have fallen in love with Ella Anderson.*

Eventually, my eyes grow heavy with sleep, and I succumb to the call. My last thoughts are of Ella. She's mine and I will take care of her. Always. That's my promise to her. *My actions will speak louder than words.*

CHAPTER 11
GRAYSON

As I stand at the crimson- and black-colored podium in the high school stadium, a sense of peace comes over me.   This is the moment I've been waiting so many years for, the time I've been longing to come and now here it is.   The colossal stadium is jam-packed full of family and friends of our graduating class of one hundred and twenty-one students. *Wow.*

I glance up to the *"Blackwood"* family section decorated with 'congrats' signs and dotted with our school colors of red, white, and black.   I'm immediately humbled by such love and devotion.   My entire family is here to watch me walk across the stage and accept my diploma.   One of many I hope to achieve.

I gaze at the different faces I've known all my life, full of pride, *for me.*   My sisters, Fallyn, Jo, Sage, and Addie, are looking down at me, tears glistening in each one of their eyes.   Their families are here as well, which makes this moment even sweeter, more special.   I notice my father's face is one mixed with pride and distraction. *Not gonna touch that today.*   My mom's expression radiates love and hope.   I catch a glimpse of my grandma, who looks identical to the rest of my family. And sitting right beside her on the end of the row is the most beautiful girl I've ever seen, my Ella. My breath catches from her perfection.

I'm instantly thrown back to the night we shared together at prom. Her soft moans of pleasure, the way her body formed to mine, it was amazing. Feeling Mr. Big Shot start to grow, I tamper down those thoughts...*another time*. I thank the man upstairs and the graduating committee for the oversized graduation gown and smile to myself.

Ella and I have been inseparable since that night. Afterwards, it seemed a dam had burst, bringing forth all her feelings and mine. Even though there hasn't been anything else physical between us since that night, we formed an unbreakable bond, it seemed. One forged out of love, passion, and respect. However, the downer is, my father is not happy with the situation. He complains about her using my family's wealth and status to help her dad's new business. The fact that Ella's father is mysterious and rumors are that he is dealing drugs doesn't help either. Ella doesn't realize the extent of my family's worth.

"Hummm," I hear a voice of someone clearing his throat, drawing me back into to the present.

Seeing the principal staring at me shifts me into gear and I gather my thoughts, proceeding with my speech. After all, that's what the Valedictorian does...*and that's me*!

"I'll be perfectly honest...no advice will be given in this speech," I start my words of wisdom to my classmates. "However, what you take away from it is up to you."

A hush goes through the stadium as all eyes are trained on me, watching and listening intently as I carry on for the next ten minutes, joking and making my point.

Coming to the end of my speech, the next words I speak really hit home for me. Writing this speech was hard, but when the *Giving Tree* by Shel Silverstein came to mind, I had to use it. It transported me back to a wonderful memory of my sister Jocelyn reading to me. She loved books and wanted all of us to share that love.

"All of us have heard the story of the Giving Tree, the selfless tree that graciously offered a young boy everything he wanted—branches to swing from, apples to snack on, shade to sit in. As the boy grew older, he began to request more, and in an act of self-sacrifice, the tree allowed the boy to cut her down and use the wood to build a boat and sail away. Many years later, the boy, now an old man, returns and the tree ... now nothing but a severed stump, says, 'I have nothing left to give you.' For a fleeting moment, the tree felt what it was like to be carefree and not have to worry about what others thought of her ... to be universally loved ... but for doing so, she paid the ultimate price ...becoming forgotten and used. Like the tree, we too have been given gifts we sometimes overlook and take for granted: education, experience, extremely good looks." I smile into the crowd for a second to accentuate my point.

I continue after the laughs die down. "With these gifts comes the responsibility of choice. We alone decide how our talents are bestowed upon the world—to either further our *own* interests and passions, or to gain the momentary approval of our peers and cohorts. This is our destiny, and we hold it in the palm of our hands. As you embark on the rest of your life, I urge you to do what you love...Because those who mind don't matter, and those who matter don't mind. Thank you and congratulations!!!"

Cheers, hoots, and hollers erupt throughout the stadium, and my time on the platform is at an end. I glance back to my family and give my biggest, brightest smile, just for them. *I did it!*

* * *

Walking into the house, I'm met with a round of applause and cheers coming from my family. Looking around, I touch eyes with each one of my sisters. Their faces are still so giddy, I cringe at their happiness.

Then I see *him*, my father, standing as still as a statue at the back of the crowded room. Dressed in his dark pinstripe suit with his favorite Stetson and snakeskin boots, he gives me a nod. *Is that his approval?* Maybe. I can't be sure. It's surreal. In his own way, he's acknowledging me, well done. *Wow! I didn't expect that.* Glancing away without further thought of him, I put on my best smile for the ones I love.

My graduation party is in full swing, my friends and family mingling and engaging in conversations. Lights are strung up throughout the gigantic living area. A table full of every one of my faves lines the outer wall, which I'm drawn to. Taking Ella by the hand, I head toward the food. *I need to eat!*

After we fill our plates to the rim, I lead Ella to an empty spot right beside Sage and her new husband, Lukas. She's tall in the lady department herself at five foot nine inches, but Sage's husband towers over her by a foot. I'm a tall one myself at six foot two, but Lukas is a tower at six foot seven, with a heart as silly as a child's. A gentle giant. *Or that's what Sage always says!*

As we sit down, Sage looks up at me with my same-colored eyes. I'm struck by how much we favor each other, even when I never thought so before. It was always considered the three older sisters look similar, carried the same features. As for Addie and I, we look a lot more alike than the rest. But looking at Sage, I have to pause. *We all do look alike.*

I shake my head when Sage begins to talk, "Hey bro, you know how very proud I am of you...I mean, Lukas and I. I can't believe you finally crossed that line, and West Point...pretty cool! The sky's the limit."

Feeling shy all of a sudden, I answer, "Yeah, I guess so. I'll be leaving in three weeks, can you believe it, Sage? Only three more weeks left of living here and I'm out." I hear a grunt beside her and see Lukas eyeing me with approval.

"We all knew you could do it, little man, umm, I mean you're not so little anymore, but you know what I'm saying. Just always remember that you *need* to do whatever makes you happy, Grayson, and fuck the rest!" She smiles at me fondly, full of mischief and love.

"Thanks, sis." I lean over and put my hand on hers. A moment passes between us. Our eyes reminisce back to the sadness, happiness, and something else is there in her eyes that I'd never seen before. Shaking it off, I know what she's saying without saying it aloud. *Fuck him!*

Seeing that Ella is finished with her food, I rise to take our plates to the kitchen, leaving Ella in good hands with Sage.

Approaching the kitchen, I see Jocelyn and her husband, Keagan, are huddled together affectionately in a sweet, loving embrace. Keagan is a big son-of-a-bitch, though he's not as tall as Lukas, towering over me only by an inch or two, but that's not what makes him huge. He has muscles everywhere, sculpted by years of military service and his current line of work. Although, if his bald head and goatee didn't create a menacing aura, his eyes always give me pause. Piercing, ultramarine blue that seem to glimpse into the soul.

Jo looks up at me. "Oh, hey, Gray. I didn't realize you were standing there." My sister uses the nickname she gave me so many years ago.

I smile back down at her and understand. It took a while for her and Keagan to arrive at the place they are today. They fought hard to have the loving bond they share. So I can't say anything to hurt her. Instead, I start my picking.

"Well, maybe you should get a room?" I joke with her.

She blushes instantly and I know Keagan's steely gaze is on me. Not wanting to ruin the moment, I ignore it, because this is what Jo and I do. Hearing the chair move, my attention is directed toward Keagan. Unfolding himself from the chair, he approaches me, holding out his hand.

I nervously take his hand in a manly shake and hug. "We're all so proud of the person you've become, Grayson. So damn proud of you. I look forward to seeing more of the man," Keagan praises. "I'm gonna go talk to Ollie for a few minutes. Trident business never ends."

Before I can say anything else, he reaches down and places a soft, sensual kiss on Jo's lips. The man can be a bear most of the time, but he loves his woman. It gives my heart hope.

Going around to the empty chair, I sit down beside Jocelyn. Instantly, she reaches out to grab my hand, pulling it to her mouth for a sweet kiss.

"I loved your speech tonight, baby brother. It was beautiful." Jo sighs and I know she's referring to my reference of the Giving Tree.

"I knew you would, Jo. You gave that to me. Fueled my love of reading, escaping to so many different places while never leaving my room." I pause for a second.

"Those nights I read to you are some of my most cherished memories, Gray. It still hurts so badly that I had to leave you and Addie. I'm glad I gave you something of me though."

I feel the anguish in her voice, because like my other two sisters before me, we all have those 'fond' memories of living at home. *Not!*

"So proud of you, Gray. Just one word of advice though..." she whispers. "I see the way you look at Ella and the way she looks at you. I've seen that look with Fallyn and Oliver, me and Keagan, even Sage and Lukas. Be careful. You have to find a way to accept yourself first, forgive others, and heal before you can make any kind of commitment to anyone else." She takes a breath and immediately, I'm inundated with so many emotions.

"Don't look at me that way, honey. I'm just saying, I know you, Gray. The real you. You have so much to offer the world and someone special," she accentuates the last part.

"It won't happen overnight, baby brother. Look at the rest of us. But just know that it can and will happen. I love you so much, Grayson Taylor Blackwood."

Knowing what my sister says is the truth, I lean over, placing a gentle brotherly kiss on her cheek and wrapping my arms around her in a heartfelt embrace.

"I love you too, JoJo!"

After everyone is full and the conversations begin to meld together, Fallyn heads to the piano in the corner of the room. The anticipation is building, because we all know what's about to happen. My sisters and I gather in the center. One of our favorite pastimes is singing together. Creating a beautiful melody for our enjoyment. Expressing our love and dedication to each other. I've grabbed my guitar, Jo, Sage, and Addie have the microphones, and the piano begins to play a favorite tune. We sing and dance into the wee hours of the night. Enjoying my sisters and their special gift of time.

CHAPTER 12

Leaving in two weeks, I sigh half-heartedly to myself. It's only been a week since graduation, and time is beginning to close in on me.

Ella is snuggled up close to me on the couch at her house, the heat from my body seeping into her colder one. My dreams are finally coming true. I'm leaving the View and going to West Point. But for reasons of this beautiful girl curled up in my arms, I'm sad.

"Penny for your thoughts?" Ella asks.

"Just thinking how perfect this moment is, right now, with you, Bluebird," I begin to explain.

She smiles up at me with her beautiful pools of ocean blues, the ones that make me crazy and stir my hunger at the same time. Leaning in to give her a delicious kiss, I stop when my phone starts to go off. Startling me at first, I reach over and see my mom's number. I give Ella one quick kiss and pick up the phone.

"Grayson, thank goodness," mom breathes.

She seems distraught, and I'm promptly on alert. "What's wrong?"

"It's your grandma, son. She's....We need you to come down to the hospital," she chokes out on a sob.

Jumping up off the couch, I begin to pace back and forth across the small living room. "What is it? Just tell me!" I shout louder than intended into my phone.

"She fell last night at home, and you know she was alone. When your Uncle Danny went by to check on her this morning, she was…" the sound is cut off by a blood-curdling cry. At that I know it is bad.

"I'll be right there, momma," I hang up the phone and peer over at Ella, who is sitting attentively, waiting for the bad news to fall.

"It's my grandma, Ella. She's at the hospital, and I have to go now," I explain as I anxiously connect our eyes.

She gets up without saying a word, grabs her purse as she goes, and we walk out the door together. *Oh God, please,* I silently pray. *Please let my grandma be okay.*

When we arrive at the hospital, we are shuffled into to a private waiting room with other family members. The room is full as I make my way toward mom. Fallyn is on the floor with Sage, holding hands, as Jo rushes forward to embrace me. No words are said. It's eerily quiet for so many people in this tiny space. Sniffles coming from Jo catch my attention, and I know everyone is waiting for news on how grandma is doing. Ella makes her way to my mom and before long, she is leaving the room to find coffee for everyone. We've been here for a few hours, and there has been no update. My worst fears keep invading my head, and the longer we wait, the harder it is to fight them.

That's when Dr. Peaden walks in and relays the events of the last few hours. "Polly Jean, Wood, Becka, your mother had extensive damage to her heart and we weren't able to resuscitate her the last time. She arrived unconscious, barely breathing, and never regained awareness. We fought hard, but her heart couldn't take the amount of stress she was under. I'm really sorry for your loss."

Wailing begins and panic grows to an all-time level. Denial is in the air. No one wanted to believe their matriarch was gone. The woman who was the glue that held the family together all these years has left us all, leaving behind an emptiness that can never be filled.

I'm stunned. Helplessness begins to set in my bones. *Why didn't I check on her last night?*

My father stands up from across the room and heads toward our group. I cringe when his arms circle mom. She's beside herself with grief, and he doesn't like displays of emotions, especially in public. I notice the subtle pressure he uses on her shoulders, and my anger explodes. Her crying becomes a painful moan.

I jump toward them to interrupt the torment he's causing her, only I'm too late. Keagan intercedes and is softly holding my mom in a hug. I see that Ollie and Lukas are standing in front of me, creating a barrier between my father and Keagan. A united front, an alliance forged to usurp the evil this monster generates towards his family. Now their family.

Ella

A week later, the funeral is about to begin. Grayson and I arrive at First Baptist Church and are met by Grayson's youngest sister, Addie. Tears streaming down her face, she rushes into his arms, crying hysterically. "She's gone. She's gone." Over and over she repeats the litany. Peering up at Grayson, I witness the anguish and turmoil as the pain hits him again. He collapses into a pew with Addie on his lap and soothes her by rocking her back and forth, murmuring words of comfort.

Slowly, one by one family members begin to gather around us. Not knowing how to help, I remain silent. When Mr. Blackwood enters the area, everyone's attention is directed at his words, "Brother Bill will be directing the service. We've requested that Ollie speak for the family." He nods toward Fallyn's husband. "She will be missed, but we have to remember we represent the Blackwood Family name today and we do not want to shame her memory."

His words were not of comfort but a sharp reminder of the Blackwood legacy. It contradicts the beautiful person I grew to love over the past year. Matilda Blackwood shone her emotions and love from the inside out. It was never a secret of the love she had for her family. The life she built and lived for.

GRAYSON
(This Is Our Life #1)

The church is completely full with only standing room left as people come to pay their respects to the woman lying in the casket. As the organ begins to play soulful gospel music, the mourners quietly wait for the service to start.

After the service, everyone gathers at Matilda's home. The front door has become a revolving door, and people I've never met shake my hand and hug me, wishing their best condolences. It was too much to bear. Just finally getting to know Grayson's family, my heart was breaking.

A fine line between the families is drawn. Aunt Polly Jean and Aunt Becka huddle together with their families. There's no love lost between the siblings. Each wants their share of the Blackwood fortune. Even though Wood is the only son and had been left the bulk of it when his father passed, Matilda's estate is substantial in its own rights.

Heading outside, my eyes land on Grayson sitting on a swing by himself. He motions me forward and captures me in his arms. "I can't believe she's gone. I don't know what I'm going to do without her."

"What would she do, Grayson? She would mourn and then she would tell you to get your ass in gear, because your life is just beginning and you've got work to do. You leave soon, and her dream was for you to go to West Point, graduate, and serve in the army. Do something with your life away from the ranch." I gently remind him, "You promised."

Softly caressing my arm, he nods. "I will keep my promise. It's so sudden. I thought she would always be here and now...she's gone. She's really gone."

Nothing else needs to be said. Wrapping him up in an embrace he so desperately needs, I sit quietly with him, listening to the trickling sounds of the pond, whispering and soothing his battered soul.

CHAPTER 13

GRAYSON

Hoorah! Duty, Honor, and Country—my new motto. Today my dream begins. West Point. *Here I come.* The clock on the wall is blaring at me, sending my whole body into meltdown mode. I leave in eight hours, thirty-two minutes, and twenty-nine seconds...*deep breaths*.

My mom is having a hard time letting me go. We talked late into the night. I held her tightly as she cried about her loss. She knows I won't be back for a long time and understands it's time to let her little boy go. It doesn't stop me from worrying about her and Addie, not having me here to protect them. I have to believe in my sisters. They promised me they would take care of them. That's why they've moved back to the View. I know my family has it under control. It's my turn to leave.

My Bluebird's not going with me. Part of me will be staying in Florida until we're together again. Knowing this is the right move for me, my mind's telling me '*Hell yeah,*' while my heart is screaming '*Don't go.*'

We've been inseparable the last few weeks. She's been my rock. Seeing her upset almost changed my fortitude, but I know we can't have a future without me following my dream. This is for the best. She's my zing and I'm not giving her up. Ever.

We said our good-bye's last night after having dinner with my family. One of the hardest moments was when she started crying.

"I'm sorry, Grayson. It just isn't fair. Just when we've found each other, now I'm losing you."

"Shhh, little Bluebird. You know that's not true. I will come back for you. You can count on that. I'll never give you up," I hold her tightly, smelling strawberries and vanilla.

We're sitting on the bed of my truck under the stars, cuddled up close, out in the field at the end of my driveway. Even with the thick summer humidity in the air causing stickiness on our skin, we don't want to separate. Wrapping her up in my arms as her tears flow freely down her face guts me. I gently lay her back onto the padded blanket I've spread over the back of my truck. Wanting to show her my words are real, my actions speak for me.

I kiss her deeply, guiding her shirt up and over her head as the dampness of Ella's body clings to the fabric. Once off, she moves to help me take off mine. We startle as headlights approach and the rumble of a truck is getting closer. Ella quickly puts her shirt back on. Leaning up, I see who it is...my father.

He exits the truck and approaches us. "What are you doing here, boy? Your momma is looking everywhere for you."

"Just spending some time with my girl. Before I leave."

"Well, hurry up, Grayson. Momma's waiting." He grumbles as he makes his way back to his truck and leaves. Typical dad. Our time is cut short and I take Ella home.

Getting up from bed to finish packing my suitcase, I'm interrupted by Addie's knock on my bedroom door. Her baby doll eyes are glistening with tears. "Now, Adalyn Grace, we've talked about this, and you're not keeping your part of our bargain. No tears. No crying. You promised, baby girl. I'll be back next spring. Just think how great Christmas will be around here when you are the only kid Santa visits," I laugh, trying to gain a smile from her. As I reach for her, she bats my arm away and continues across the room to sit in the rocking chair. Once seated, she looks at me, trying hard not to smile. She's so temperamental lately. Her mood swings go from cold to hot in five seconds flat. She's got that Blackwood temper and is not afraid to use it. She will be very dangerous to the male population soon. God help them all.

"Christmas won't be the same and you know it. It will suck! And just because I'm the only kid doesn't mean I'll get more. Gosh, why can't you stay here and go to the community college? Why do you have to go so far away? Oh yeah, and why can't I talk to you for six whole gosh darn months? I've never gone one day without talking to you. You're asking way too much of me, Gray. You're not just my big bro, you're my BFF," she pauses to take a deep breath then continues, "My life's gonna suck monkey toes without you. You know that. Mom's clingy and dad... Well, he's dad. He's never interested in anything I do. I've got horseback riding competition starting soon too! Who's gonna give me advice about boys? You do realize that I'm almost thirteen, right? Well, I'll be dating, and my big bro won't be here to take care of me... I could go on and on, but you get the point, right?" Grumbling, she stares out the window to the pasture and starts laughing.

Turning my head to see what has her giggling, movement catches my eye when Razor, our Australian Shepherd, scrunches low on his hind legs as he stalks a rabbit on the hill. He pauses periodically, frozen in time with his front paw lifted up along with his tail and ears. Silly dog. He looks hilarious as he stalks his prey. His timing is perfect, because it gives me a moment to collect my thoughts. I love Addie and don't want to hurt her feelings, but she's really being selfish at the moment. I'm not abandoning her; I'm going to college. It's part of life. We've always made her the center of our universe because she's the youngest, but this is just too much. Even for me.

"Are you finished bitchin', yet? This is temporary. Just like grandma always told us, it's another chapter in my book of life and I don't want to miss it, Addie. I might not be here physically, but you know my heart will be with you. Write me, and I'll write back. Six months isn't forever. You keep practicing and I'll be back before you know it. Fallyn, Jo, and Sage are here for you too." I shake my head in exasperation at her final plea for me not to leave.

Glancing at the clock one more time, I hear a bustling down the hall and Fallyn appears in the doorway.

"You 'bout ready to go? We've got a drive to get you to Mobile in time to fly out. Why in the world you made your reservation to fly from there is beyond me. What in the hell were you thinking?" she adds as she grabs my suitcase and wheels it down the hall. She didn't even give me enough time to reply. This ride should be oh so much fun.

Looking around my room one more time, I motion Addie forward. She takes her time crossing the room and into my arms. As we hug, moisture begins to pool in my eyes and I know it's time to take my leave.

"I love you, Adalyn Grace Blackwood. Good journey till we meet again," I quote He-Man from the Masters of the Universe, one of the many movies we've watched together over and over on nights she couldn't fall asleep.

Riding to the airport with Fallyn is a true test of my will. *Who in the hell taught her to drive?* She's driving pedal to the metal like Dale Earnhardt, Jr., her most beloved racecar driver, while Bon Jovi blares *Livin' On a Prayer* over the radio. Crazy woman, she's gonna get a ticket.

"You know we have four hours till I have to be at the airport, right? And it like takes only two and half hours for a normal person to get from the ranch to there. You could slow down a little, Fallyn." She grunts at my comment, not replying. I try again, "So, why ya in such a hurry, Little Lyn?" I use my pet name for her. She cut it short to make it easier on me when I was little and couldn't pronounce the F in her name, and I tacked the little on when I eventually outgrew her small five-foot frame.

"No hurry, no worry. I promised I'd get you there and I will. Don't want to let you down, G," she states while swerving in between vehicles. My stomach does not like this and if she doesn't stop soon, I'm going to throw up in her nice little Lexus!

Fallyn is the strong one of the group. She's like a mother hen! She keeps us all together and doesn't allow weakness. She only asks of you what she is willing to give. She left home when I was two years old. Our relationship has always been strained because of dad. He ran her off and she never stopped to look back. Don't get me wrong, I love my sister, but sometimes I wish it could have been different from the beginning.

All of a sudden, her car begins to beep, signaling a police car up ahead, and she finally slows down.

"Looks like ya got your wish, Grayson, you must've been praying really hard," she jokes. "Are you ready for your next chapter to begin? It can be overwhelming starting over in a new place, not knowing anyone. Most folks want to stay close to home, but I guess we aren't like most people, are we, hon? You'll be fine. I guarantee it. When I left home, the hardest part was not having my family around. Many a night I cried myself to sleep, wishing I had y'all close, but I kept on telling myself it was temporary, and finally lo and behold, it was over and done and well, you know the rest. You can do this, you're a survivor, you carry the Blackwood name."

No other words were better said. She knew what I needed to hear, and I thank God for her words of wisdom—Fallyn style.

We arrive at the airport and Fallyn parks the car in order to help me find my way. This is the first time I've flown by myself and I'm a little anxious. People from various places around the world are hustling to and fro, scurrying to their next checkpoint. Chaos in a controlled environment. You can feel the excitement build as she escorts me to the final line that begins my journey away from family and friends.

As we exchange hugs, she reminds me, "Even when you don't think you can, you will. Dig deep and keep going. Don't listen to other people and never ever care what they think or say. Keep yourself safe, young one, and know the force is with you," she uses a mantra shared between us as a reminder they've got my back.

Once I board the plane and locate my seat, the

countdown continues while the plane waits on the runway for take-off. The stewardess is droning on and on about safety belts and exit locations.

I locate my iPod and select a playlist for my journey. My thoughts begin to drift and I'm wondering what my beautiful Ella is doing right now. Is she thinking about me? She vowed to wait for me and I promised to come back to her. So much can change in four years and long-distance relationships are famously known for failing miserably. Are we the exception? I'm doing this for us. For our future. Only my gut tells me it will be different. I can't turn out like my old man. I want more than wading in cow shit all my life. I want to see the world and leave my mark on it.

As I fervently whisper in my mind over and over *'Sweet Ella, wait for me,'* the plane starts its ascension into the sky and my new beginning.

CHAPTER 14
GRAYSON

Seven Years Later.

It's hot as hell! Sweat is pouring down my back from the intense heat of the sun the afternoon supplies in the Middle East. Driving into the middle of a warzone is not what I'd call a good day. The truth is, this place buries its way into the soul, digging its sharp talons in, making it hard to break free. Free, such a small word with a profound meaning. That's why we're here, for the freedom of the people in this God forsaken place, and for the protection of our own country.

It's been two years since I was assigned my team. *That's right, my team.* I finished up at the academy earlier than expected and was immediately sworn into the army. My work ethic, grades, and leadership caught the attention of Colonel Carl Wilson. He approached me before graduation and I became a member of an elite special operations unit. After the ceremony, I was thrust into the fray and sent over to the Middle East. It was my dream come true. The hard work and sacrifice paid off. *Good times...Hoorah!*

The horrid smells of gunpowder and imminent death plague my senses. The sky is a sandy yellow haze tinged with the onset of the blistery, setting sun, reminding me again this isn't home. Glancing at the perimeter around the truck, I notice a few things look off and my inborn senses trip my internal alarm. My heart is pounding wildly in my chest, warning of danger ahead. Shadows dance off the glass windowpanes from the surrounding abandoned buildings. We continue to drive through the mostly empty streets, and the further we proceed, the more my gut goes crazy. My instincts are never wrong. They've kept me alive. Honed from a young age. Something's not right.

The uneasiness continues as we inch closer to the designation point. I glance at Beauty and Aabdar sitting in the backseat. We found Aabdar through contacts of contacts. He's a native and knows these streets and people well, and loyalty can sway quickly with the right incentive. For the last three months, he's been our point of contact with members of the terrorist cell we are currently targeting for intel. When our caravan nears the next intersection, I notice a shiny reflection on the top of the building and my unease intensifies. Turning back, I grab the informant's shirt, "What the fuck?"

I signal to Beauty, my second-in-command and interpreter, to relay my comment to this piece of shit. *Yeah, I said Beauty.* He got his name real quick because he's such a looker. A mountain of a man with olive skin and dark green eyes emitting strength and provoking fear, he's really scary. *Get your head in the game, Grayson.*

As his strong jaw flexes and eyes narrow on the

informant, Beauty rattles Aabdar with questions, and his voice escalates. Beauty knows my looks, signs, silent messages even before I speak them. That's why he's my second. From the get-go, we clicked. Creating an unstoppable force while adding to the dynamics of our team. He continues to press the shaking man, finally getting him to spill everything. His right eyebrow shoots up, capturing my eyes. Knowing this is a sign to me. *Fuck, not good.*

"It's a TRAP," Beauty and I both roar. "Check your six!" I relay by com to the men in the HMMWVs (High Mobility Multipurpose Wheeled Vehicle-Humvee) following in front and behind us.

Next, all hell breaks loose and our convoy is rocked off its axis. The deafening boom of a bomb explodes on the left side of our vehicle. The impact lifts the Humvee up off the ground as if it's a toy car, twisting slightly before slamming back down with a bone shattering jar. My ears ring loudly as a buzz pounds through my head, temporarily dazed, while smoke and dust billow throughout the interior. After wiping the dust and sweat from my eyes, I snap alert, searching my scope for the assailants. I catch sight of Aabdar as he's yelling and kicking while being dragged out of the truck by several armed men wearing turbans around their faces.

Gathering my bearings, I muster the strength to crawl from the crumpled vehicle, feeling the bite of rubble scraping my hands and knees as I continue to be aware of what's going on. Scanning the vicinity, I see the other two Humvees in a strategic blockade maneuver. Boxing us in for protection. Beauty nears and I signal him closer as I relay my command, "Fuck! Light 'em up! Get those motherfuckers!" I bellow out to my team.

Like a battle cry in the night, bullets whisk and ping around us, trapping the team in place. We begin a strategic maneuver, each individually working as one. Preparing to strike back against the terrorists. Beauty scrambles to gather equipment from the vehicles, placing them ready for use and powering off rounds as he does. In stealth mode, Styx rounds the back transport, setting up for his assault on the hostiles. Animal gains ground up around the front of our makeshift barrier, organizing his equipment for execution. Without further thought, instincts kick in and my team is lost in the assault, doing what we've been trained to do. Kick some motherfucking ass!

Tossing a grenade into the fray of insurgents, Styx readies for action as the enemy scatters for cover in the deserted buildings like the cockroaches they are. Pushing through the falling debris and raining dust, he runs into the spreading crowd, fighting his way to our informant, using only his knife and fists. We all cover his move, capping off anyone who poses a threat to our team member. It's an amazing sight to see when Styx scoops up Aabdar in a fireman's hold without breaking speed and proceeds back around to our secure location.

Then we're falling back into the building fifteen feet

away from our barrier that Radar cleared during the conflict. We gain additional cover as Styx releases another grenade toward the opening of the building, where the enemy took cover. Keeping our eyes on the area around us, we shuffle into the building, slamming the door as the sound of gunfire lingers in the air.

We take a minute to catch our breaths. "Major pucker factor, boys!" Beauty calls out as he surveys the entry and exit points.

"Hoorah!" echoes through the open space.

"Don't get comfy just yet," I order my team. "Radar, get on the horn and let base command know our location and that our cover is blown. We're FUBAR."

The men instantly go into field strip mode, taking stock in ammo, checking their guns and tending to any wounds that need attention. We are privy to the best equipment and protective gear money can buy, but sometimes bullets stray or gashes and cuts happen. And after the bullshit we just wrapped up, no one's that lucky.

Jacobs a.k.a. Doc, the team medic, begins to clean a few wounds Styx received during his crazy ass stunt. Nothing deep or life threatening, thank God. Jacobs is the quietest one of our tight-knit group. Lethal in all areas and never hesitates, just like the rest of us, but he also has a calming, healing nature that helps in times like these.

Johnny a.k.a. Animal I've known all my life. My best bud. Instead of following his dream and becoming a vet, Johnny decided to enlist in the military. He moved through the ranks quickly and became one of the best snipers around. I knew he would be part of the team I was building; it was a no-brainer. He's someone who has always had my back. Now we're working together.

Styx is our explosive expert and one crazy son of a bitch. Case in point with him jumping into the fire, but that's what we're best at, assessing the situation and rectifying it. Pete, a.k.a. Styx, and I've been friends since high school. Pete graduated with Johnny and me. He played ball with us. He was one crazy motherfucker then. Styx loved to blow shit up, on and off the field. I was surprised as fuck to find out he was a candidate for my team. Another one I trust implicitly.

"Your hands are so gentle, Jacobs. That feels real nice, man." Styx murmurs in his sexy voice, and we all begin to smother our laughter.

"Shut the fuck up, man," Jacobs calmly states without pausing even for a moment while bandaging Styx's arm. No longer able to contain it, they erupt with laughter.

I chuckle under my breath at the little exchange between my men. That's the whole of it, my team. Even in the hellish situation we're in, they can still find a little humor. It's so important to stay sane in this wretched desert, a combat zone. Since we're special ops, we spend a lot of time gaining intel, waiting, and like today, fighting in the middle of chaos. It's times like these I tend to take stock, thinking back and wondering how my family's doing, where my Ella is...

My mind drifts back seven years to the letter I received from Ella two months after I left home.

Dear Grayson,

I'm sorry to do this in a letter, but I just didn't think I could wait any longer to tell you. I can't wait for you, Grayson. You should move on too.

Good-bye,
Ella

Three fucking sentences are all she gave me. My Dear John letter. At the time it hurt so bad, although we never claimed 'I love yous', she is my zing. I tried to find her when I went home for the summer, but it was like she had vanished into thin air, and her dad was worthless in gaining any information. I've never gotten over her. She still haunts my dreams. *Not now, Grayson. Enough!*

Gaining back reality, I shake off thoughts that will get me killed and address my team. "Radar, what's the status of our extraction?"

We need to get out of here before daylight breaks and fatigue sets in. We can rest in shifts, but not knowing how many men are lurking outside doesn't bode well for an extended period of time.

"We've been told to take cover and salvage what we

can from the wrecked Humvee." He proceeds, "There's a Bradley convoy moving out to arrive at zero two hundred and we'll follow them out." He looks down and continues typing on the laptop. "Coordinates to our position have been relayed."

Radar was a child genius. Computers are his first language. Why he decided to become a soldier and not the next Steve Jobs is beyond me. He graduated from MIT at the young age of twenty and his skills have been sought after by many corporations around the world. I'm sure there's a story behind his decision to be a soldier, just not sure what it is. He's a very private person; only giving details necessary for the performance of our team.

"Unless the hostiles pose a bigger threat, then we'll need an extraction chopper ASAP," Beauty joins in before he takes a sip from a hydration pack.

"We'll cross that bridge when we get there. No need to ask for trouble. Right now, we sit and wait," I calmly state and pull my knees to my chest to rest my aching head on. "Embrace the suck. Johnny, you take first watch."

Darkness surrounds us in the infrared-lit building. Only the whites of our eyes are glowing, a faint red is visible. We're hunkered down, waiting for extraction. Taking a deep breath and inhaling the stench of mold tickling my sand caked nostrils, the only thing I can think of is how nice an ice-cold beer would be right about now.

GRAYSON
(This Is Our Life #1)

Game time. Sometime later, Radar signals to me, conveying the incoming convoy is almost here, which ignites the team into a rush of adrenaline and anticipation. "Lock and load 'em, boys. It's extraction time," my whisper covers my team via coms. Gathering up our gear, locking our guns down tight, we crouch low, preparing to leave the place of refuge we had found. No noise is heard from the other side of the door.

Signaling again with a nod of his head, Radar gestures the time is now. Exiting single file, we hug the wall of the darkened building, no shadows and complete silence. A vehicle is close; the noise of the engine is faint. The Humvees sit in the distance, unmanned and ready.

I motion for Styx and Jacobs to begin moving Aabdar toward the nearest one. Silently, Beauty leads the remainder of the team and I'm flanking the rear. Everyone is in position as the Bradley thunders onto the street, indicating it's time for action. Gunfire erupts. As we break for the Humvees, adrenaline is high, filling me with a sense of comfort I always get during these fucked-up situations. We begin cramming into the vehicles for cover as the Bradley team shields our movement.

Bullets sail around through the air, whizzing by my head and legs when a harsh jolt rackets me forward, followed by a sweltering pain. I'm knocked off balance for a brief second then jump into the awaiting Humvee.

F. G. ADAMS

The smell of copper assaults my nose. I look down to see blood gushing from a wound. "I'm hit!" I grunt from the pain now searing freely through my body.

CHAPTER 15
Ella

"Ella, Ella Bo Bella Banana Fanna Fo Fella Mi My Mo Mella, Ella," sings Savannah as she enters the break room in the emergency room department set up by the army in the middle of the fucking Middle East. "Where's your Dr. McDreamy on this glorious day in the desert?" she inquires while shuffling back and forth between doing the bump and smurfing to the song in her head.

Laughing at the display and echoing her choice of greeting, I rap, "He's gone, gone baby, down by the poolside," and join in on the dance. We are causing a stir, judging by the stares we receive from the newbies doing their clinicals. "He left after his shift to quote 'chill by the pool until I get off later today.'" I mimic his earlier facial expressions, causing another round of giggles from us.

"Ain't life just grand? Lucky little devil," she continues. "If I had a stud muffin like you, I would be taking my leave and finding the closest hammock in the oasis of life." She wiggles her eyebrows up and down. "Bet he's got one hell of a yummy popsicle!"

"Damn girl, don't you have a filter? And, um, hell yes, I rather like his popsicle too." Winking, I continue,

"And one day you'll find your special flavor," I state.

It's been five years since my graduation and I've spent them as a soldier and nurse in the United States Army. Savannah and I met in basic training and have been inseparable. The girl's a nut! She hails from Texas, where they grow 'em bigger, if you get my meaning, or so she tells me quite frequently.

The day I met her, we had finished a five-mile run. I was spent and the drill sergeant in charge wanted more. I almost quit until she got in my face and told me under no uncertain terms, she was not gonna be the only girl left in this platoon and for me to buck it up. Needless to say, I did, and from that moment on we've been the best of friends.

She pulled me out of my depression. After losing my mom my senior year in high school, my dad up and moved us about forty-five miles west of Lakeview, only to move back once I left home. My options were limited and I decided to opt out of my last year in high school and enroll in a fast-track program at the community college. Within eighteen months, I graduated with my Associates in nursing. The ROTC program allowed my commission into the army as an officer.

To make matters worse, not only did I lose my mom, but I lost my first love, Grayson Blackwood. I received a letter from him a couple of months after he left for West Point, stating he had met someone new and hoped I would understand that a long-distance relationship wouldn't work and blah blah blah. I never looked back. After graduation, I gathered the few things mom had left me and enlisted. It was my one-way ticket out of the View. Evan followed my lead and is now serving in the navy.

As I finish my chicken salad, Savannah nudges my arm. "Would you look at that piece of eye-candy walking through the door. Um, um, good. Think I'll mosey on over and see if I can get his name, rank, and digits," she cackles, gathers her trash, and heads toward her newest victim.

Savannah is drop-dead gorgeous and can drive a man to drink with her sassy mouth. Sometimes it amazes me that we are best friends. She's the opposite of me. She has snow-white hair cut short, accenting her pear-shaped face and mossy green eyes. I have long, curly dishwater-blond hair and almond-shaped blue eyes. She's a perfect ten with an hourglass shape and long, long legs. I'm shorter with a badonkadonk and only a handful of boobs. She's loud, obnoxiously funny, and doesn't know a stranger, while I enjoy sitting back, watching people, blending with the crowd. I guess it's true when they say opposites attract.

Bets run high with our crew on how long Savannah can keep a guy. Kind of like how to lose a guy in ten days. So far, her longest streak has been eight days. Maybe she can set a new record soon. She's been burned in the past, thus her rule of no attachments allowed. I know that feeling. *Been there, done that.*

Before we shipped off on our third tour of duty, Savannah and I went on a double blind date as a game of dare several of the soldiers shared. That's how I met Lieutenant Colonel Michael Barnes. He was the first man I'd been attracted to since Grayson. He was his complete opposite. Tall, dark, and handsome describes the yummy man I'm engaged to. He tempted me with his raven, mussed hair and smoky blue eyes, and before I realized it, we were a couple. Savannah's date, First Lieutenant Steve Rogers, is now one of our best buds. They didn't make it past two days before accepting it wasn't gonna work out for them as lovers.

Exiting the break room, I begin my rounds checking on my patients.

An alarm begins blaring over the intercom and a voice sounds off, "Incoming injured. Possible gunshot wounds. No fatalities known." We scurry around, readying the operating rooms for the next patient. Everyone knows their job and we are prepared when the helicopter lands and the injured soldiers are being wheeled down the long corridor toward the operating rooms. Preliminary diagnostics are being done on the fly as we evaluate and disperse.

CHAPTER 16
GRAYSON

Drifting aimlessly, the air of euphoria saturates my body. The next moment, my feet set down on solid ground. Not solid, but warm, sinking sand. *Where am I?* Looking around cautiously, I notice I'm at the beach, lying on a blanket, and right beside me is Ella. *What the fuck?* Bluebird snuggles close to my aching body, causing a ripple of peace to rush through me. She peeks up at me with those beautiful blue eyes and mutters, "Grayson, we're a hundred miles away from the nearest army base." *Wait, what?*

The bumpy movement of the vehicle lurches me awake from my semi-unconsciousness as we make our way further from the deserted town and armed men hunting us. The ache and pain caused from the shock of the bullet entry had sent me into a blackness laced with old memories, and I'm not sure how long I've been out. Noticing the golden sun rising from the east is an indication that it's been a while and responsibilities for my team seeps into my mind. My head throbs when I try to raise myself from the prone position. The unyielding rock of a seat reminds me that my body hurts and soreness has set in, but I'm familiar with pain and can endure it. I hear Beauty mention to Johnny that we are a hundred miles away from the nearest army base with hospital care. Knowing we are heading that way, I request, "Status?"

Answering automatically, Beauty responds, "A base camp due west of our position for medical. Aabdar and you require medical care, stat." Steely determination laces his words.

As if on cue, Radar's voice cracks over the com, offering more details on Aabdar's status.

He was shot during the abstraction, and Jacobs finally reduced the blood flow. The evac chopper is meeting in fifteen minutes at the rendezvous point to take the wounded. *Yeah, that'd be me. Fuck!*

"Follow to safe zone and await orders," I mumble, fighting the pain and weariness taking over my mind. "We need intel from Aabdar. What the hell happened back there? We were set up. Figure it out, boys. Need answers yesterday."

The chopper appears in the endless blue sky up ahead, descending toward a vacant spot to temporarily land. The metal tail swivels left to right, finding balance to perch on the solid ground. There are no trees in this desolate stretch of land we are traveling, nothing but endless amounts of gritty sand. Dust plums in the air from the twirling propellers as we wait for it to calm enough to depart.

Medics rush to the first Humvee, where Aabdar is located. He is lifted to a waiting transfer board. He's unconscious and not moving. *Not good. We need answers.* The attendants run toward the chopper with him in tow, securing him for flight as an onboard flight medic starts an IV.

They come back to my Humvee. I'm lifted from the back seat and strapped securely to be carried toward the whirlybird. I clench my jaw painfully from the movement. I'm ready for some good medicine to staunch the aches and pains. A needle pierces my skin and an icy sensation sweeps up my arm. Instantly, the heat from outside dissipates and my eyelids become heavy. The rocking of the bird lulls me to sleep as we lift off the desert floor and accelerate to our destination.

A white light is blinding me when I try to open my eyes. "Hello, handsome," a gentle voice says. *What the fuck?*

"You're a little groggy from the anesthesia, aren't you, hon? No problem. You're in recovery. Do you remember you were shot in the shoulder? Nothing serious really. A few stitches to seal the hole, and the doc said you'd be good as new. You'll be up and outta here in no time flat, big boy," she comments. *Nothing serious, my ass.*

"Where am I? Where's my team?" I inquire. The voice I hear coming from my mouth is cracking and barely above a whisper. My shoulder is throbbing as my head starts to clear. I try to unclog the frog that's taken root in my throat. "How long have I been out?

She gives me a quirky smile. "Hold your horses, baby cakes. First off, you're at the medical center. You came in earlier this morning with another injured soldier. As to where your hunk-o-lious team is, they're in the waiting room," she giggles softly as she brings a straw to my dry lips. I gulp greedily like a parched animal. "Not so fast there, cowboy, don't want that coming back up."

I watch as she stands from the stool, sits the cup down on the table, and writes something on a clipboard. She's humming a song that seems familiar, but I can't name it. She's way too happy to be in here with me. I need answers now.

"When can I see my team?" Feeling a little less thirsty, I ask, not worrying that anger has seeped through my voice. I'm getting pissed at her nonchalant attitude. This chick is hot as hell and definitely not playing with a full deck of cards.

She continues from the end of the hospital bed and starts taking my vitals. "As soon as we move you to a room, they can visit. Anxious, are we?" She bats her eyes, using her hand to fan her face. Ignoring her, I remain silent.

The hospital room door opens and the doctor walks forward. Glancing up from the chart in her hands, she grins, "Hello Captain Blackwood, I'm Doctor Kyla Calloway glad you're back with us. When you arrived, you were a little out of it. Loss of blood, no doubt. The bullet entered your upper shoulder. In and out. No nerve damage. You were very lucky, soldier. We cleaned and stitched both the entry and exit wounds.

You will take it easy for the next fourteen days. We will re-evaluate then when you can return to your field assignment. Any questions?" she asks, heading back to the door.

"How long do I have to stay here? I've got men depending on me."

"You will be released in the next three to five days. You can return to desk duty then until you are fully released." Her left brunette eyebrow rises, soliciting further questions. She nods and she's gone.

"She's a whirlwind, but one of the best doctors we have," the nurse says.

I had forgotten she was in the room. "Let's see if they have a room readied yet and get ya moved. Sound good, sugar?" She leaves the room and finally, I'm left alone.

Replaying the events in my mind, little inconsistencies are noted. A plan forms. I need Beauty. He'll be my eyes and ears for now.

CHAPTER 17
Ella

Waking up snug and cozy in Michael's arms comforts the little girl inside me, her need for stability that was missing as a child. Groggily rubbing the sleep from my eyes, I turn to see he's staring at me. With a smile plastered across his face, he leans in and whispers, "Good morning, beautiful," capturing my lips in a sizzling kiss. Out of habit in our normal routine, he proceeds to untangle from our embrace to fetch our morning coffee. I watch his muscular ass on display as he leaves the bedroom naked. *Perfect.* He is *sex on a stick* as Savannah likes to say.

When he returns with our coffee in hand and reaches out to hand me one, I sigh. "You are too good to me, Michael." He settles back down on his side of the bed and we drink our coffee while silence surrounds us, giving ourselves time to wake up as my mind drifts back to the previous night.

Michael was upset when I came home so late, not at me really, but the situation. He had made a special dinner for us. When I walked in, the candles were barely-lit wax spreading out at the bottom of the holder. Cold, untouched plates of Chicken Alfredo with bread sticks were sitting on the dining room table. Sitting quietly on the leather sofa, he was agitated with dejection written all over his handsome face. I couldn't blame him after all the trouble he went through making our favorite meal. Clearly, he changed his tune when he found out what was going down at the hospital. But that was Michael; he could get his feelings hurt and quickly recover. Easy to forgive, forget, and forge ahead. Never taking any moment for granted.

I resigned myself a long time ago that moving on from my past and Grayson was the only way to survive. After the letter he sent...*not going there.* Then meeting Dr. Michael Barnes, I had a chance to heal. The friendship between us was undeniable, and the rest followed. Not the fireworks I felt with Grayson, but it was pleasant. We share a comfortable passion that appeases my restless soul.

"So, what would like to do today, babe?" Hearing his voice startles me out of wandering thoughts.

"Honestly? I'd just like to hang out around here for a little while. I'm still so tired from the long, crazy day yesterday," I reply to his sweet voice.

"Okay, babe. Whatever makes you happy." Sitting his coffee cup on the bedside table, he maneuvers his tall, lanky body to the end of the bed, kissing my legs as he goes. He snatches my feet in his big, capable hands and massages them thoroughly. *Mmmmm.* He knows what I need.

Instead of going out later as planned, we decide to stay in for the rest of the afternoon. Lounging around in our pajamas in comfortable companionship. Michael brushing my hair from my eyes and showering sweet kisses all over my face, while we quietly read on the cushy sofa, was just what the doctor ordered!

Savannah called later in the afternoon to ask if she could come over and play cards 'or something' as she put it. She's always in need of friend action when not on the prowl for a man a.k.a. sex buddy. *She's crazy to the highest power! Love it!* Because I can't say no to her, we get ready for the impromptu evening of fun and games. Michael called Steve to come join in the fun as well. Knowing Savannah wouldn't mind even though they had tried and failed at a relationship; we're all still good friends.

Sitting around the dining table, snacking on pizza, drinking beer, and taking shots of Jack Daniels while playing Cards Against Humanity has to be the pinnacle of my week. The game Savannah brought, CAH is extremely vulgar, hilarious, and fun as hell. Taking turns, the person drawing the black card, better known as the Czar, asks a question. Then everyone else chooses a white card from their own deck that they deem the funniest, craziest answer. Shock factor wins every time. The Czar picks one winner, everyone else has to take a shot. Needless to say, Savannah and Steve seem to be winning big time.

Finally, my turn to be the Czar comes, and the card I pick up makes me blush with the innuendos and answers that are sure to follow.

"Okay...blank is a slippery slope that leads to blank," laughter erupts from all of us. Savannah, Steve, and Mike all hand me their two white cards.

"Alrighty, here we go." I read the first set of cards. "<u>Shaft</u> is a slippery slope that leads to <u>balls</u>. Good one. <u>Menstruation</u> is a slippery slope that leads to <u>shutting the fuck up!</u> Really nice." My laughter is getting out of control a bit. "Last one. <u>Mutually-assured destruction</u> is a slippery slope that leads to <u>getting your dick stuck in a Chinese finger trap with another dick</u>. Oh my." At this point, we are all rolling over in the chairs. Laughing it up. *Good times.* The Chinese finger trap wins! Of course, those were Steve's cards, so Savannah and Michael took their shot of whiskey, while I only had to watch.

We play for a while longer, taking a break to get more food and bathroom breaks. I go into the kitchen to grab more pizza when Savannah comes in after me.

"So...oh, my fucking goodness, I just have to tell you about the wounded soldier at the hospital," she's whispering under her breath. "He is oh so delicious and H-A-W-T, hot, hot, hot."

I look at her, puzzled for a moment, wondering where all this is coming from, but it's Savannah, so I listen intently as she finishes what she has to say.

"He's a Captain too. Oohlala! I'd like to giddy-up onto his saddle, if you know what I mean," she ends with bump and grind movements that send us into a round of giggles and snorts.

We continue to play the game, getting shit-faced, loving every minute of it. At the end of the game, Savannah and Steve take their leave. Since we all live in the same complex, I know they'll be safe walking back to their living quarters.

Two days later, I'm back at the medical facility, getting ready for my shift. When I grab the first chart of the day, an arm circles my waist and a gentle kiss is placed on my neck. It's Michael. We walk down the long white clinical hallway toward the first door on the right, stopping outside the door. He places a kiss on my lips, "See you at home in the morning, babe," as he continues toward his office to prepare for his rounds.

Dazed by the sweetness of Michael's gesture, I walk into my first patient's room and stop dead in my tracks. I'm met with a pair of piercing amber-colored eyes staring straight at me. *No way! It can't be. After all these years. It's him. It's Grayson.* My heart rate accelerates as memories flood my mind.

"Bluebird?" His husky voice reaches out to wrap around my fluttering heart. Time stands still, and for a brief moment, I travel home...to the View with Grayson. Then the slamming of an outside door jolts me back to reality and the moment is gone.

Turning around, I rush toward the door. I have to escape now. I won't survive another bout of Grayson Blackwood.

CHAPTER 18
GRAYSON

Boredom started the moment I refused the pain medication the staff had provided for my shoulder and my head cleared. I prefer my senses alert. I can handle the pain. It's not an intense burning now unless I move the wrong way. Even then it's tolerable. Nothing an 800mg Ibuprofen won't take care of. The doctor visited last night and mentioned possibly releasing me today. I want out of here.

Not one to idly sit around, I know the shit storm that hit the fan the moment General Fox caught wind of the situation over here. Accountability for walking into a trap hangs over my head. Hearing the door open, thinking the doctor plans to make good on her promise that I am healing fine and can leave this place, my stare collides with the heavenly eyes of my dreams. "Bluebird?"

After all these years, she walks back into my life and I'm lying in this shit hole, my arm in a fucking sling, wearing a hospital gown with my ass hanging out. My body thrusts forward, trying to reach her, but she turns away and runs out the door without a word. *What was that about? Was that really her?* Maybe I'm seeing things in my overworked brain and the recurrent state of pain I'm in right now.

The door swings back open a few seconds later. *Did she come back?* No. Not that lucky. It's that crazy ass nurse, Savannah, wearing a peculiar expression on her face.

"How are you doing today, Captain? Ready to bust out of this joint?" she questions and reaches toward my arm, adjusting the blood pressure cuff. "What'd you do? Your heartbeat is racing a mile a minute."

"Not sure what's causing it. Must be the fucking medicine. Been doing nothing but counting the cracks in the ceiling." Pausing dramatically and pointing to the first crack, I begin counting, "One, two, three…"

Ignoring me, she continues, "Sure thing, sugar. Is that why Ella ran outta here like she just got a visit from the Grim Reaper?" she remarks in a mocking tone.

"Twelve, thirteen…"

I'm not about to discuss Ella with anybody, much less her work associate *if* it was her. Fucking A. My curiosity is getting the better of me. Analyzing the situation and redirecting this fucking conversation to benefit me, I conclude maybe it wouldn't be bad to know more. I *need* to know more.

Breaking the silence, I ask, "Ella Anderson?"

She glances downward and nods affirmation. "She's been stationed here the last five months. One of the best folks I know. You know her?"

"Yeah, something like that. We went to high school together. It's been a while, so I wasn't sure if it was

Blue...um, I mean her." I slam my mouth closed after that blunder.

The door opens and a doctor I haven't seen before walks toward the side of my hospital bed. Savannah smiles at him and comments, "Oh there's the man of the hour. Hi, Doctor Barnes. Thanks for letting us crash on you and Ella last night." Oh, fuck no! *What did she just say?*

She's watching my reaction. I'm careful not to show any emotions on my face, but inside, my gut churns at the mention of Ella with someone. *She's mine.* Barnes talks to Savannah, and I take the opportunity to study him. Tall, lanky build, black hair with a strong Romanesque face. Brainiac. He exudes confidence just standing in the room. Straightaway, I don't like him. He has something that belongs to me. And I know I need more intel. For now, he's become my newest target.

"Well, Captain, everything looks good to go. I'll have the paperwork started for your discharge. With any luck, you'll be out of here by lunch," Barnes notes, pausing and scribbling something on my chart as he leaves the room.

Savannah sighs and I wonder what's next. I don't have to wait long. She says, "Ella's more than a former classmate...isn't she, sugar," and follows the path out the door.

What did I think? That Ella would wait around until I found her? *Stupid luck, Grayson.* Seven long years

I've been away from her, not a word or any way of finding her. She vanished. And of all the fucking hospitals all over the world, she just happened to walk into mine. An army nurse at that. What are the fucking chances? Later. I'll get my chance to talk to her.

Dressed in fatigues with my arm strapped in a matching green sling, I'm pacing the room, waiting for departure. I'm still pacing an hour later when Johnny, Beauty, and Styx come strolling in.

"Your chariot awaits, my king," Styx jokes, pushing a wheelchair and stopping in front of me.

"No fucking way am I leaving here in that," I spit out.

"You will if you want to leave, sugar," Savannah commands, walking from behind Styx. She's checking him out. Her eyes are roaming all over Styx, and he's enjoying every minute of her perusal. When she meets his glare, it's his turn, and it isn't a casual glance. No, he stakes a claim on her body and the pleasures awaiting her later. He's letting her know what to expect from him, and by their looks, they have come to a mutual agreement with no words necessary.

When their sensual exchange ends, Styx pleads, "Come on, Captain. We're going to visit Aabdar before we take you to your temporary quarters. It's not like we all haven't gone for a ride in one of these before. My ass has seen so many it would put your ass to shame."

I look at Johnny and Beauty for moral support, but the grins they are sporting help me realize they're not going to be of any assistance. Motherfuckers! No negotiation here. It's a losing battle, so I concede and sit down to the joy ride. *Well, shit! Yee-haw!*

There's no sign of Ella as we leave my room and head to the elevator. A small glance at her would ease the beast's restlessness I'm fighting with inside. After seeing her, I know rest is not an option until she's in my arms again, where she belongs. Convincing her will be a challenge, but I will be the victor. Failure is not an option.

Quietly, Styx wheels me into Aabdar's room. A single fluorescent glow shining above the bed is the main source of light in the tiny room. It's sparsely furnished with only the hospital bed and a chair. His body is propped at an odd angle. I'm shocked at what I see; he's hooked up to so many machines. It's only been three days since he was almost captured and then shot in the back. He's got a long way to go before he will be back on his feet. The bullet had to be removed and internal damage repaired. He's one lucky son of a bitch to be alive. His face is swollen with black and blue bruises, a white bandage wraps around his forehead and left eye. Several cuts and scratches on his bare arms are visible from his struggle during the raid. A tube is protruding from his mouth as a machine beeps in the background.

"What's his status?" I ask the attending nurse.

"Captain, he's in a medically induced coma, sir. The doctors feel the pain would be too intense for him to remain still. He requires time for the internal stitches to heal, sir."

Beauty continues, questioning her as to when he could possibly wake up. Looks like it will be at least fourteen days. *Fuck!* I'm responsible. What happened to him should have been avoided.

Something isn't settling with the chain of events from our supposed meeting with Mustafa, lead man of the large terrorist group. No one knew about the meeting location and time except Aabdar, my team, and his second in command of the terrorist cell. We had kept it secretive for this very reason. The more people aware, the less it could be contained.

My head's screaming that Aabdar is the likely culprit, but why would he walk into the trap with the knowledge he would die? It doesn't fit. He's not a fanatical and seemed level-headed from the start of the operation. His family weighs heavy as his responsibility. He has four children under the age of ten, and is the only source of income and protection. No. I don't believe it was him.

I'll keep my mind open for the possibility, but a nagging thought continues to sway me in another direction. It's time for contact. I'll make arrangements for a secure transmission as soon as I'm settled in my new quarters. General Fox needs to be aware of the situation. With the nurse reassuring me she would call immediately when he wakes, we head out.

CHAPTER 19

Ella

Air. I need air. I rush out of the room and bump right into Savannah. "What's the hurry, sista?" she asks as she catches the chart that fell from my hands.

"I can't...I can't do it, Vanna. I need," I gasp for breath, "I need some air. You have to take care of this patient," I whisper through my deep inhalations to Savannah as I turn away and quickly walk down the hallway away from her, *away from him.* I hear her calling for me to stop, but I can't, not right now.

Taking the stairs two at a time as if the devil himself is hot on my heels, I head up to the roof. With my heart pounding wildly in my chest, I escape through the double doors onto the second story and begin breathing erratically. *I've got to calm down.* Being almost eight thousand miles from Lakeview, I should be protected from the onslaught of ever laying my eyes on Grayson Blackwood again. *Why? After all this time? It can't be him.*

For seven long years I've been trying to eradicate the pain that comes with thinking about Grayson.

At first, I was crushed beyond recognition. I didn't want to get out of bed, brush my teeth, go to school. Everyday, normal things were a chore on my crumpled heart. I was crushed. There were so many unanswered questions, things left unsaid. He had promised me. Promised he would be back, vowed we would be together again. *Promised me that I was his.*

Unwillingly, my eyes glisten, remembering the last words he spoke to me the night before he left my world.

"You're my Bluebird, my zing, Ella. I belong to you and you belong to me. Always."

A pledge stopped short a few months later by the letter he sent me. *Stupid.* So a week later, proceeded by a whole bunch of cookies 'n cream ice cream along with my mother's insightful lectures and hugs, I was picking myself up to move on.

Then mom died a month later, which threw me into a whole new spiral of despair and grief. Even when you know death is imminent, you still aren't prepared for the emotional roller coaster spin. To make matters worse, my mom was gone, and the boy I fell in love with escaped my grasp. Darkness was my friend.

My dad decided we had to move right after the funeral, so we packed up and left. What could I do but follow? I didn't care anyway; everything I loved was gone.

The day before we left, I stopped by to see Addie and say good-bye to her. I made it a point to keep in touch with her after Grayson left, although I hadn't seen her since the letter. She didn't know, I'm sure. It wasn't her fault.

GRAYSON
(This Is Our Life #1)

When I arrived at the Blackwood ranch, Mr. Blackwood was outside on the porch. Immediately, I wanted to turn around and run, but digging deep, I faced one of the scariest men I'd ever met. Harold Blackwood—better known as Wood—stood up as I approached. His mixed river-moss blue eyes held mine as his mouth turned into a fine, thin line. 'He doesn't want me here,' blared in my head.

"Well hello, Miss Anderson. What brings you here today?" he growled out the snarky question that I know was not a welcome greeting.

"I was..I was hoping to see Addie, um, Adalyn for a few minutes. I'm leaving town tomorrow and just wanted to say good-bye." I felt the nervousness bubbling up through my voice.

With a satisfied grunt and nod, Wood went back to looking out over his vast homestead. I made my way to the house and said good-bye to Addie and Mrs. Blackwood. Their sadness and longing bled in each of the words they spoke.

"Ella, we'll miss seeing you. I wish you didn't have to go." Addie said, stifling a sob as tears welled up in her eyes. "Please come back and visit when you can."

I left Blackwood ranch that day with a heavy heart, entering my newest adventure, but never to return, never to see Grayson Blackwood again.

Coming back to reality, I feel tears streaming from my eyes. My vision is blurry and my heart is aching.

I'm over Grayson Taylor Blackwood. I have Michael. He's perfect for me. He makes me happy. *Then why am I bawling my eyes out? I'm just in shock, yeah, that has to be it, right?*

"Great," sniff, sniff, "now I'm asking myself questions?" My body is a stark contradiction to what my head is saying.

I hear the metal door swing open and close with a loud bang. Tensing, I frantically wipe the tears away, because whoever is approaching will instantly know by my reddened face and swollen eyes I've been crying.

Soft, feminine arms encircle me, filling my now parched form. *Savannah.*

"Hey, honey. Shhh. It's okay. I'm here." She calmly brushes my hair away from my tear-stained face with one hand while holding me tightly with her other one.

Crying as Savannah holds me helps my raw heart. Her next words stop my dreadful blubbering.

"Does blue mean anything to you?" She gazes down at me with earnest. "Well, honey pot, I knew the moment I laid eyes on him that it was the infamous Grayson Blackwood before even taking a peek at the chart. You know I'm curious about this man from your past. He started to call you blue but stopped."

My throat closes up and I can't speak. *He still calls me Bluebird. That's what he said when I walked in the room.* Clearing my throat, I nod my head with nothing to say.

GRAYSON
(This Is Our Life #1)

Savannah sighs. "I *see*, Ellie pie." She accentuates the word see. A fresh round of tears spills down my face, and Savannah takes a deep breath.

"Listen, sugar, everything will be fine. He's being discharged as we speak. There'll be no need concerning your cute self with him anymore. We'll just stuff those worms right back in the can, 'kay? It's over and done. He's leaving, so no muss no fuss," she finishes off her statement with a hint of sadness in her eyes.

My head acknowledges what she's saying...out of sight, out of mind. Although with that mourning comes the fact that today I got a glimpse of the man, not the boy. My body was on fire the moment our eyes touched. Even through the bandages and hospital garb I could see the well-toned muscles of a hard body and his sculpted, matured face made my heart stop. All those old memories and emotions crashed down on me again. *What am I going to do?*

Finishing up all my rounds, I avoid the room Grayson was in or may still be in. *Ugh! I'm a mess.* I make it home with just enough strength left to shower and crawl into bed. Michael wouldn't be home until the early morning because of his rotation.

Longing and grief bombard my every pore. What I wouldn't give for Michael to be here to put his strong, soothing arms around me, caressing me, whispering to me that everything would be fine. *Michael.* I can't tell him about this. There really isn't a 'this.' For now, I'll try to bury those feelings and memories. Besides. Like

Savannah said earlier, he's checked out. Hopefully to never return.

Being alone with my thoughts is very dangerous. I'm tossing and turning in my bed, the same bed I share with Michael. But my mind keeps drifting back to Grayson. I should be ashamed. I shouldn't think about him, not here, not ever.

The brain is an interesting organ. It can invoke pain, grief, happiness; so many emotions, even pleasure. And right now, flashes of prom have hijacked my imagination.

"You don't have to say anything, Ella. Just let me love you. Even if it's just for this one special night," he whispered. "Let me show you how much you're wanted and what you do to me." I feel his tongue caressing my clit. I'm soaring. My body no longer belongs to me. It's his. Pleasure crawls up my spine, through my body in a massive feeling of bliss. My stomach tightens, and I begin to fall into mind-blowing pleasure.

I clench my eyes tightly, my body aching for a release from the memories. Too far gone as the lost accounts of Grayson's touch assault my senses. Memories I've kept locked up tight, forgotten, touch my aching heart. I move my hand slowly down my aching body to my silky Victoria Secrets and slide my fingers between the material and flesh. Caressing the hood at first, my fingers extend lower into the hot wetness seeping from my pussy. Rhythmically using the juices my body is providing, I paint gentle circles on my clit, dipping inside my slit, triggering small contractions around my fingers. Mimicking Grayson's cock. All the while my mind races for a glimpse of the ecstasy I felt when Grayson touched me. Not wanting the feeling to end, I pull my fingers out and start all over again.

My breathing labors from the rush of pleasure and the tightening in my belly. With my other hand, I caress my nipples. They're hard and distended. I am lost in the illusion of Grayson stroking, sucking, and touching me. Panting as goosebumps crawl up my flesh, I thrust my fingers in and out, in and out, while my other hand lowers to my clit. The pleasure continues as I near the edge of oblivion. Each stroke takes me closer. Moans fill the silence and my body explodes. Ripples of pleasure tingle all over, soaring from the orgasm my body so desperately seeks.

Sometime later, my labored breaths are gone and I'm left empty again...and thinking about Grayson. The fire was lit again and I'm not sure I can extinguish the burn this time. *I'm in big trouble...yep!*

CHAPTER 20
GRAYSON

"Yes, sir. I will continue as planned until further notice. My objective hasn't changed. I'll get the intel required. It may take longer than anticipated, but I won't fail. Thank you, General." I disconnect the satellite connection with General Colin Fox.

It's been five days since I was discharged from the hospital and had to wait for an audience with the General. Apparently, there has been more happening around the world to other special operation teams than just mine. We have been infiltrating smaller terrorist cells for several years, and our efforts have paid off many times over. The happenings on September 11th ignited our resilience to fight terrorism and secure our Nation's freedom for its people. We are reminded daily of the lives lost, civilians and brothers in arms. I was just beginning my military career, but the loss is felt just the same.

With the mission on my mind, I start plotting my plan of action with the limitations of an arm sling and stitches. Now that I know the direction the General wants me to pursue, I can assemble my team and enact a plan. My head's about to explode from the pressure of exposing the individuals responsible for the rebellion.

There are not enough rocks in this world for the troublemakers to crawl under and hide. Eventually, they will make a mistake and we will be there.

When the team arrives, we start brainstorming the most likely scenarios to bring the culprit to justice for the ambush. We're all sitting in my quarters, drinking coffee and speculating how the location of the meeting with Mustafa was leaked. We'd spent months cultivating the relationship with his cell and others in the region. Our cover was legit. Radar had made sure the trail was believable. The room isn't spacious, and chairs have been pulled together around the table as a makeshift command center.

"How're you wanting us to attack this?" Beauty opens the discussion again. "We were set up by Aabdar and I'm sure we can all agree somehow he's responsible. Being shot could be a diversion from the truth."

"He's pretty messed up, man. Not sure you're on spot with that assessment," Animal comments.

Styx adds, "Yeah, dude. He was fighting for his life when they were dragging him across the road. Not somethin' you're gonna do if it's your plan. They were stabbing him while I was pulling him out of their clutches. They didn't want to let him go alive."

"His wounds were significant. He's lucky to be alive," Doc inserts. "Maybe he was set up and didn't know the extent of the plan?"

"Doesn't matter if he was part of it or not; it

happened on my watch, and I'm not gonna rest till I know the truth," I say.

"We've received confirmation for a secondary meeting site. Mustafa wants the arms. He's not letting this setback affect his business. He has a buyer and wants what we promised him. The transaction will go forward as planned," Radar mentions.

"The General wants him and his cronies served up on a platter. We'll proceed with caution. Once Aabdar is up and going, we'll get the answers. Until then, we're on alert for any suspicious happenings in the area. Beauty, you're our contact for the area. Keep your ears to the ground and find something out," I order, reminding them of the mission.

"Yes, sir. I'll put out feelers and keep you posted."

"Radar, you're our presence on the web. Do your magic and find us a trail. Something we can use to end this faster. You all have your assignments. Keep me abreast of your findings, boys." I stand, signaling the meeting is over.

I want the ones responsible for Aabdar's hospital stay. The ones who made the mistake to mess with my team. My mission and country. I want them to pay for their actions. One way or the other. We've eliminated several contacts, including Mustafa, the elusive head of the cell.

It will take time and planning. I can't have any distractions. Yet Ella keeps hounding my mind, every waking hour and even in my dreams since our brief encounter. But the threat is real, and no one is safe until this mission is complete.

* * *

Today the stitches will be removed. Beauty arrives at my temporary quarters early with black coffee and donuts. Sometimes his intuitive senses leave me staggered. He knew I would need a ride to TMC without me asking.

Beauty updates me on Radar's search for an electronic footprint among the unlimited World Wide Web, as well as the Dark Web. Something to link Mustafa with an outside seller or possible buyer. It's a needle in the haystack, but if it can be done, Radar is the one. *He uncovers it all, smart son-of-a-bitch.*

I'm anxious to possibly see Ella again. With all that's been going on, we haven't connected yet. I need to talk to her... need answers from her. The sooner, the better. I need to protect her.

Seven days, seven nights have passed since seeing my Bluebird. As soon as we walk into the hospital, I know she's here. My Ella radar is on alert. Standing back, I'm able to see the woman she has grown into. She's a looker. Fuck. Prettier than in high school. *If that's even possible.* She has a body that oozes sexual delights. Her feminine curves have developed into luscious handles that my hands ache to hold on to while ramming into her from behind. *Damn.* Her cupid lips are strawberry red and her long, curly hair is bundled on the top of her head, accentuating her neck. I'm losing focus as she turns and walks down a hallway, her hips swaying as she leaves. It takes all my willpower not to run after her.

We approach the nurse's station, sign in, and take a seat to wait for my name to be called. It doesn't take long before Savannah is there, ushering us to a room down the hall.

"How's the shoulder, Captain?" Savannah asks and helps remove the sling. "Need ya to remove your shirt, so we can get those nasty stitches out."

As I take my shirt off, she gasps and stares at the tattoo on my chest. It begins above my right pec and extends upwards over my shoulder. There are two bluebirds soaring from flaming red and yellow flowers into the sky. One is smaller than the other. The male following and protecting his female into the blazing sun ahead with a menacing scowl for others outside their world and eyes only for his mate. Their journey beginning together into an unknown world. It's Ella and me. Together. In love. Happy.

When I graduated from high school, I knew what I wanted. It took time to find the right person and several sittings with the artist to capture my vision. I was marked. For life.

Savannah is momentarily stunned. Not a word is said as tears form in her eyes. Then she knocks the wind from me. "She's engaged."

Oh hell, no! This can't be happening. I'm stuck in a nightmare and want to wake the fuck up. Now. My mood just took a nosedive from bad to raging.

"Who?" That's all I need to know. My voice is husky and raw with emotions I don't want to give away.

"Dr. Barnes." Seriously? What the fuck! Ella's forgotten my promise. "They've been together for a long time. He just recently asked her, and he makes her happy."

I make her happy. Or I did at one time. She was happy with me until I left. I need to remind her of what we shared.

"Thanks for the heads up. I got this," I murmur.

I push my emotions down deep so this woman won't know my intentions. Not yet. I'll have Ella again. I don't need any outside influences.

Savannah finishes her task and gives me instructions for the care of my healing wounds. I'm not sure what she's thinking right now, because the looks she keeps giving me are definitely not helping my wounded heart. I need to get out of here. When she's done, I dress, thank her, and head off to find Beauty.

We're walking toward the exit when my little Bluebird appears. There she is, and this time she sees me as I walk toward her. There's no running from me, even though she tries to ignore the command my eyes are sending her way. *Stay put.* Her eyes dart to the door leading to the stairs and she opens it, trying to avoid me.

"Beauty, wait for me here. I'll be right back," I command and begin pursuing Ella.

She's leaning against the wall, her head back and her eyes closed. When the door slams shut, she immediately sees me and panic settles on her beautiful face. *What have I done to cause this reaction?* Calmly, I walk toward her like I did with the young calves on the ranch, letting her know my next move. She's skittish.

"Long time no see, my little Bluebird," I try to ease into a conversation with her. "How have you been?" She's reluctant to answer, so I press on. "I've tried to find you. You moved away before I could. All my searches stopped with dead ends."

I see her vulnerability and it breaks the walls of my discipline. I reach for her, capturing her in my arms. Her body stiffens and I begin rubbing my hands up and down her back in a soothing pattern, leaning toward her succulent neck and inhaling her unique scent. Strawberries and vanilla. This feels so right. She belongs with me. My body ignites, a fire burning deep for her.

She pulls away quickly when I lay a light kiss behind her ear.

"Grayson, please don't do this..." She moves from my arms toward the exit. "I'm involved with someone. He's special to me. I care for him and would never hurt him."

Nodding and grabbing her again, I place her in my arms and declare my intentions. Renewing promises from years past.

"Bluebird, you can fly away from me as many times as you need, but I will chase you, your place is with me. I'm not giving you up. Ever. Just give us a chance. You know you are mine."

Finding her here is an omen. Paradise is with Ella. I won't let her go again now that I've found her.

Her eyes begin to falter as her resolve breaks down. "Grayson…"

The siren blares, signaling our moment is over. She's gone in a flash, pulling away from me. Duty calls. I know what was said between us was enough said to push us to the forefront. I'm patient sometimes when it's necessary. This is one of those times. She needs the reassurance that we were meant to be. As long as I'm the one she's with in the end.

CHAPTER 21
Ella

Approaching TMC in the early morning calms my beating heart. It's the time in the wee hours of daybreak that set the stage of quiet accord through the grim desert. All I can detect are the subtle sounds of a vehicle and faint whispers of helicopters moving through the sky. Peaceful.

Apprehensive ripples encircle me after another restless night spent in my bed all alone. Michael came home this morning just as I was stepping out of the shower. We're on different shifts this week. Entering the bathroom, he kissed me breathless. He took my towel and gently wiped the droplets of water away from my arms and legs before he moved to my core and most intimate areas. Paying significant attention to my breasts and my special place. Not missing a drop. I was so hot and bothered by the time he finished, I wanted to jump his bones, but the weariness in his eyes told me it would have to wait.

Also, I was feeling a little guilty for my fantasies of Grayson I've had every night since our brief encounter in his hospital room. Ultimately leading me to come so hard each and every time. *Well, shit!* I left Michael to shower and sleep. He has to be back at the hospital after lunch for surgery and needs some rest.

I push open the heavy steel doors, the blipping beeps of medical equipment along with the antiseptic smells of a hospital engulfing my senses. I trudge through another set of doors and come to the nurse's station. The smell of freshly brewed coffee tickles my nose. Walking over to make myself a cup of steaming brew, I notice Savannah coming toward me with a shadowed look on her face.

"Hey, ladybug. What's up?" I say in my cheeriest voice.

"Not much, buttercup. Long night, and I have a feeling today's going to be even longer," Savannah sighs then plasters a smile across her face. *What?* Reaching over, she takes my coffee cup right out of my hands, inhales the delicious java, and begins to sip.

"Vanna!" I giggle as her nickname leaves my mouth.

Typical Savannah. *I love this girl.* I begin to make another cup as we converse about patients and chitchat, never once mentioning the elephant in the room. *Grayson.* After we've devoured our second cup of go-go juice, it's time to start making the rounds.

"See ya later, alligator," Savannah calls over her shoulder as she heads in the opposite direction.

"After 'while, crocodile," I reply after her, forging down the stark white hallway, laughing as I go. *She knows what I need to help start my day off right!*

Functioning on autopilot, I advance from room to

room, checking in on my patients while chatting with a few wounded soldiers. I enjoy this. This is the reason I became a nurse, to help people. There is little time for my erratic meandering imagination. After grabbing some lunch, I continue with my day.

Entering the largest bay area of patients, the one where five soldiers share the space, the sounds of laughter blast through the opening door. My smile beams from ear to ear, literally sending out the message of my inspiration and love for these men. I really enjoy sharing my time with them. It amazes me that even with legs gone, arms missing, and bullet holes, this is the most positive group of guys. Men of high caliber. Knowing if they could just get out of the bed they're stuck in, they'd be back on the front lines serving.

These guys sacrifice so much every day they go into battle. Some of them never make it back, and others return with broken bodies. Not their spirits, though. The fondness for the character of each soldier I interact with gives me peace.

I'm swamped with so many emotions as I go from hospital bed to hospital bed. *Grayson could be lying in one of these beds.* I push that thought from my mind and continue checking on my guys and making small talk.

"So how are you today, Sergeant Eastman?" I lean in to wrap the blood pressure cuff around his one good arm.

Sergeant James Eastman, hailing from the great state

of New York, came in two weeks ago. He was caught in the crossfire of a pipe bomb explosion en route to give aid to a small rural village outside of Kandahar. He lost his right arm that day. When he came to TMC, all that was left of his arm was a bloody stump just below his shoulder socket. Even after he woke up, his spirit never broke. Soldiers know the risks. Sergeant Eastman was just glad to be alive.

Clearing his throat and smiling up at me, he replies with his Northern American accent, "I'm tight, ma'am. Wishing for a bodega right about now. There's one right around the corner from where I live. The coffee is sick! How 'bout you, ma'am?" He waits on my reply.

"Pretty good, thanks. I'm always good when I get to visit with you." I smile sweetly at this hero.

His wife and two baby girls are back in the Bronx in New York. He finishes telling me how he Skyped with them last night, choking up while relaying his wife's tears. My heart is in my throat from all the emotional baggage this soldier will carry home with him. However, knowing he has a good support system awaiting him helps.

We banter back and forth a little while longer, then I leave after he takes his meds.

As I'm retreating from my last patient's room, I hear a voice that stops me in my tracks. A voice that still lingers in my fantasies. Looking up, I'm captured by his penetrating stare. *Grayson.* Those amber-hued eyes are full of mischief and dominance. Catching me and pulling me in. *Oh shit! I've got to get out of here.* I glance around for the nearest exit like a nervous little rabbit. Spotting the stairwell, I scurry away, or better yet, run away from the man who haunts my dreams.

Slamming the door open then shutting it tightly behind me, I lean against the wall. I have a moment to catch my breath. *In...out...in...out...* Hearing the door open and smack shut, I open my eyes to Grayson approaching me carefully. *No, no, no, no, no!* I begin to panic and look around for another escape. There's no way out. Grayson is now blocking my only pathway.

As he advances on me and crowds my space, I hear him call me 'my little Bluebird.' Bits and pieces of his conversation register in my brain. "I've tried to find you...dead ends." All the while he caresses my arms, soothing my soul. Then my body betrays me as I ignite into a thousand particles of electrical charges spiked with passion as Grayson drops his head to my bare neck, giving me a soft whisper kiss behind my ear. A simple kiss I realize I've missed desperately.

Snatching myself back to the real world, I pull myself together, dissolving Grayson's grasp. *Get it together, Ella! Think about Michael...* I gather what's left of my resolve and make my way toward the door. Stopping only to tell him we can't do this.

"I'm involved with someone. I care for him and would never hurt him. This can never happen between us. Our time has passed, Grayson." I utilize as much steel in my voice as possible, but only convey my sadness.

Determination fills his chestnut eyes as he captures me yet again. Wrapped up in his warm embrace, I'm submerged in the spicy, male scent that only belongs to Grayson. The earthy flavors I've missed. My body heats up with a longing desire from the pleasures only Grayson can quench. He speaks the words, memorable words, using my pet name that will haunt me forever.

"Bluebird, you can fly away from me as many times as you need, but I will chase you, your place is with me. You know you are mine."

The emotion in Grayson's voice gives me pause. *How can he say this? He broke that promise a long, long time ago.*

For a brief instant, shivers of bliss rush throughout me just as the blaring of the siren comes over the coms. Shaking my head from the high being near Grayson has caused, I sever the connection between us. *This isn't right. I can't do this to Michael.* I give Grayson one more look, conveying everything he means to me and how at the same time this can never happen again, then I exit the stairwell. Leaving behind the one man who will ever truly own my heart.

Meanwhile...

Hiding in the shadows, Bahadur awaits. *Holy Allah. This wasn't supposed to go down like this. Everything was carefully planned. In. Out. The bastard is too smart. I underestimated him.* Talking quietly into the earpiece using the native language of the region, he says, "The Captain will cause problems for us."

He listens intently to the caller on the other end. "It can still be salvaged. There is another way to circumvent the enemy. Patience," the caller continues to fill him in on the new offense being concocted.

This proposal is so heinous it causes the hairs on the back of his neck to stand on end from the ripple of evil coursing through his veins. Bahadur breathes a heavy sigh. "Yes, I understand. I've waited many years, what's a little more time."

He laughs to himself as he disconnects the call. Another plan set into motion to capture the astute army Captain.

CHAPTER 22
GRAYSON

My mind is a mess. I'm stuck sitting in this fucking meeting and concentration isn't possible. I'm on a conference call again with General Fox and his staff. Plotting our next move against the terrorist cell we've been infiltrating here. Guns. This entire ordeal centers around controlling the shipments of arms in this area. Speculation, theories regarding our ambush, and the cause for it fly around the room. We are the suppliers, and attacking wouldn't benefit Mustafa and his gang.

Yet, all I have thought about for days is Ella. Ella. Ella. She's in my every waking thought, and it's really starting to wear me down. I need her. I need her to want me again.

I've never lost faith that one day we would be together. When I received my Dear John letter, I never gave up hope of finding her and demanding answers, answers only she could provide. Sure, I've dated other women over the years, but the thought of Ella always stopped me from taking the next step. Obviously, she didn't have that problem. She's with Dr. Barnes now. How am I going to help her remember our promises?

I learned at an early age how to deal with pain. It was survival of the fittest, where the weak fell by the wayside and only the strong survived. I saw it with the animals on the ranch and felt it with the punishment my father dosed out. Even with all that, the thought of someone else touching what is mine rips my soul into pieces.

I remember how she felt in my arms. The completeness she evoked. I want that again, and nothing is going to stop me. Not even Ella's stubborn self. She will succumb to my will, one way or another. I just need to figure out how to do that.

A throat clears and I realize everyone is looking at me. Vaguely remembering what we we're talking about, I acknowledge and the conversation keeps going. Shortly after, we break and head to TMC to visit Aabdar. Hopefully, he will be awake and shed some light on the events.

Beauty and Styx are with me as we enter Aabdar's room at TMC. He's improved since our last visit. He looks like a street fighter after a bout with an angry gorilla, and I'm furious as fuck! The bandages around his head have been removed, and the bruises are a violent purple and blue. His eyes bulge from the sockets as his eyelids begin to move back and forth.

I think he's waking as he mumbles a word that stops me dead in my tracks, "Traitor."

What does he mean? Traitor. One word. Is it someone in the ranks of the cell or is it more? Someone I know?

I glance behind me at Beauty and Styx wearing

frowns, concern etched on their faces. A noise catches my attention, and I'm turning around again as Aabdar begins to struggle as the nurse quickly inserts a sedative into his IV. I had wondered why his arms were strapped down. It seemed odd, but watching him fight the bonds as he is trapped in his nightmare justifies the extreme precaution.

"Has this been happening often?" I direct my gaze to his nurse.

Nodding, he replies, "Yes, sir. We are bringing him out of the medically induced coma. His consciousness is returning slowly. Another few days and he will be awake and aware. Right now, he's fighting to wake up, sir."

"What have you heard?"

"Nothing that makes sense. Something 'bout a traitor and an ambush. Everything else has been garbled words we couldn't understand."

"Here's my cell number. Call me if he says anything new. No matter the time. It's imperative you call me. It could be a matter of life and death."

"Yes, sir," the nurse chants.

I signal for the guys to follow me as we exit the room.

CHAPTER 23

Ella

Leaving TMC for the evening after the latest incoming wounded are tended and settled, Savannah and I head over to the gym. We call it the gym, but really it's just a mobile home on steroids. Fixed up with state-of-the-art workout equipment. You get what you get in the desert!

I know that something is on Savannah's mind due to her lack of conversation. Every comment I make she diverts with a shrug or a haughty, short laugh. *So not like her.* Not wanting to dig too deep because of my encounter with Grayson and not ready to spill, I let it go. We settle into our routine and climb onto the treadmills. Side by side we run for a few miles. *I needed this.* I needed to clear my head so I can think rationally about everything that went down with Grayson.

Finally, I can't keep it inside anymore. Needing my BFF's advice, I let loose the events in the stairwell the other day.

"So...what do you think, Vanna?" I lay it all out for her scrutiny.

Watching her face as she gathers her infinite wisdom, I could swear she seems sad. *What does that mean?*

"Don't leave me hangin', Savannah! I can't take it," I breathe out in a huff.

With an extremely long inhale she says, "Well, Ella Bella...I just don't know what to say, honestly." Again, I see the sadness in her eyes. *What is going on?*

I continue on trying to rationalize the mess I'm in now. "I know that I love Michael. He's been there for me and helped me heal. But seeing Grayson again, it's brought back so many memories. It's like I can't even breathe anymore," I mutter out as I take a deep breath.

Noticing my anxiety is buzzing wildly, Savannah stops her reps and puts down the weight she was curling. She walks over to me and puts her arms around me in a warm, loving embrace. *Just what I needed.* Although with the comfort come the tears. I wipe at my eyes furiously and chastise my behavior in the middle of a room full of people. *I've gotta pull myself together.* She smiles that beautiful Savannah smile and goes back to her weights as if saying 'enough said', leaving me to continue mine.

Finishing up the rest of our workout in silence doesn't help my battered heart. The conversation I had with Grayson plays over and over in my mind. None of it makes any sense to me. He ended our relationship. He told me to move on. I need answers, and Grayson is the only one who can give those to me. Can I ask him? Should I even bother? I have a great man in my life. A man, who is willing to give me the world when I become his wife. It's not far off from the hearts and flowers kind of love I always dreamed of, yet it's enough. He's my comfort zone. Although isn't that what Grayson told me before he left? He was leaving to make a life for *us*. And the way Grayson's touch felt was electrical, zapping my defenses bit by little bit. Like coming home. *No! I'm not going to think like that. It's not fair!* I'm so confused and the quiet is killing me.

Clearly, I've had enough of it. "Are you ready to go?" I ask Savannah in a mournful tone while reaching down to pick up my bag and wiping the sweat that's pouring down my head.

She shrugs back at me, "Not just yet, girly. I'm just getting into my grove." Finally, I get a cheery response out of her.

"You go ahead, Ella. I'll be a little while," she replies. "Besides, I've got my sights set on a hunk-o-licious over there." She nods her head in the direction of a guy with his back toward us who has an enormously beautiful physique doing squats with...is that 600 pounds? *Whoa!*

Before I leave, she stops me once more. "Look, Ella, I know right now things seem out of whack and wonky. But I promise you...it will all work out in the end. You'll see. Remember this though, things aren't always what they seem. Sometimes we judge before all the facts are heard. Just sayin'.'"

She leans in to give me a big hug and a kiss on my

check. *Wow! No truer words were ever spoken.*

Stunned momentarily by her words of wisdom, I leave the gym and begin walking down the path to my quarters. The hair on the back of my neck begins to stand on end; a creepiness enveloping me sets my already fluttering heart to a pound. Feeling as if someone is watching me, I sprint the rest of the way home. I unlock the door hastily, get inside, and bolt it locked again. Safe and sound. "Whew, that was freaky weird." Going into the kitchen, I grab a bottle of vodka and take a few shots to calm my nerves. Two become ten *maybe,* and the last thing I remember is being put to bed by gentle arms. *Michael.*

Over the next few days, a lot of weird things begin to happen. The feeling of being watched has intensified. Walking up and down the stairs at TMC is giving me the willies. Like when I was heading up to the roof yesterday to meet Savannah for lunch, I heard the door open down below. After making it to the top, I waited patiently to see who was behind me, but no one ever came. *Weird, right?* I mean, it's weird because that's not the first or last time it's happened.

I remind myself that I need to talk to Savannah about it, maybe even Michael. I just don't want anyone fussing about me. Although if someone is watching me, I need to tell somebody.

All caught up in my head, I run smack dab into a solid, muscular body. A startled scream leaves my lips before I even realize whose it is.

"Whoa, Bluebird. What's wrong?" Grayson's worried voice instantly relieves my chilling thoughts. "Ella, are you okay? You look like you've seen a ghost. And not just because I'm standing in front of you, either. I've seen you around here all week."

His smile broadly reaches out to his eyes, and I catch a peek at his intense dimples. *Yummy.*

Startled by the fact his hands are on me again, I say breathlessly, "Oh, my apologies, Grayson. I was just thinking about some things…" I don't want to say more.

I feel the sudden urge to spill everything to this man about the strange things happening around me.

"Excuse me. I hope I didn't hurt your arm or anything else." My eyes roam over his well-honed, chiseled body. *Damn, he grew up well. Stop it, Ella!*

He releases his hold on me and takes a step back.

"Alright, Bluebird, if that's the way you want to play it," he smirks at me. *Really?*

"Seriously, Grayson, I've just got a lot going on right now. If you'll excuse me, I need to see my next patient."

I drop my eyes to the floor because I can't handle his fierce attention. As I start to walk away, I'm stopped by his question.

"Hey, Bluebird. I'm not sure how long I'll be here, and I was wondering if maybe we could catch up. You know, just as friends. Maybe grab some dinner or something?"

His pleading eyes give me the impression that he's

bringing his game. *Just great!* I'm a sucker for Grayson and his tactics.

I let out a huge sigh, because I know this game so well. But I can't help it.

"Well, maybe. You could come by my place and we could all have dinner together or something like that." I lay it out, letting him know that Michael will be involved.

"Tell me, my little Bluebird...are you scared to be alone with me?"

There's that haughty smirk again. The old Ella rears up and I want to wipe it right off his face.

I lean in to whisper in his ear, "Nope!" popping the "P" nice and loud.

Our laughter erupts, and for a second I'm back in the View, sitting on his truck bed, sharing secrets, and busting a gut from his crazy jokes.

A quiet settles around us as I look into his eyes.

"Okay, Grayson. I'll do it. How about lunch? That's the best I can do. Even that will have to be minimal, because of the chaotic comings and goings in this place."

I take a deep breath and exhale. *What am I doing? It's just lunch*, I lash out at my wayward thoughts.

Grayson clears his throat and I'm drawn back to the man standing in front of me, not the boy I knew.

"Great. Just tell me when and where and I'll be there." He smiles appreciatively at me, a vulnerability in his eyes that tugs at my heart. *Shit!*

Before I lose what sanity I have left, I mutter, "The mess hall, right down this hallway on the right. Eleven hundred hours on Friday." Proceeding down the hall, I yell out to him, "Don't be late, Grayson."

I peek back at him and think I see something that resembles triumph. *Ha! Not this time. Game on, Grayson.*

GRAYSON

Fuck yeah! Lunch with Ella. She agreed. I head back to my living quarters for some much needed R&R. With so many thoughts flooding my head, I need to focus on the mission and the next steps in locating the traitor. What does this mean? I need more intel to get ready for this battle. My thoughts plague me.

I received an email from Radar with a trail he's located and following up on. He wants to keep this lead between us for now, and I understand because there's a leak somewhere and it needs to be plugged.

I try to catch up on work, but my head's not in the game. All I can think about is Ella and her sexy as hell pouty lips. I want her. It's been hell knowing she's close by but chooses to stay away. Disgusted with myself for showing a lack of self-discipline, I try working out with my shoulder. The throbbing is gone, and physical therapy is helping to work out the kinks. Every day I get closer to being released from desk duty.

GRAYSON
(This Is Our Life #1)

Johnny and Styx join me at the gym and we spend a few hours there. When we finish, we head to the mess hall for some grub. It's not my first choice, but food is food. We discuss a few scenarios regarding the traitor. Something has been bugging me for days, but I can't put my finger on it.

Johnny mentions the bullet wound. "You know it missed Aabdar's heart by a millimeter and the entry was close range. I've studied the x-rays, and the trajectory is almost a face-to-face entry."

Just when I think matters couldn't be crazier...it happens.

"Huh? That's fucked up. I've been racking my brain trying to remember the attack, every detail about the extraction. Nothing adds up. I remember parts and pieces, partly from being shot myself," I mumble my frustrations. "It's a waitin' game, fellas, and we all know the drill. We wait for Aabdar to wake and then make our move."

After dinner, we decide to meet early tomorrow morning with the team. Shower and bed. I'm exhausted. The stress from the past few weeks have finally caught up. And I need Ella.

I knew in high school she was the one, and I've never forgotten. Now that I actually have a chance to talk to her, I plan on claiming her. Taking back what belongs to me. She feels the same; I could tell by the way her body reacted to mine. Every time we bump into each other or talk briefly, I can sense her resolve fading away. *But will that be enough?*

The main complication is Dr. Barnes. I don't want her to have regrets when she leaves him, because eventually she will be mine. There's no question in my mind. No doubt. Easing her into my arms and out of his won't be easy. But I'm a patient man. I've waited this long for Ella.

I head for the shower to wash away the grime and filth from the unyielding desert and my intense work out. Turning the water on, I wait until it heats up, leaning down to take off my combat boots and slide down my fatigues. I grasp the back of my shirt with my good arm, taking care not to tug too hard on my partially healed shoulder. Left completely naked except for my dog tags, I step under the relaxing spray in an effort to lessen the pounding ache in my chest.

My thoughts return to seeing Ella earlier. Holding her sweet body close to me. Her smell intoxicated me. The memory from the past of her soft body entwined with mine and her moans of pleasure fill my senses. Before long, a yearning need stirs within me. *Yeah, I'm horny as fuck.*

Leaning back against the tile, my head falls forward into the raining water flowing down my chest. Droplets of water cascade down my abs as I reach for my hardened cock, gripping the protruding member hard. Sliding my hand from root to tip. Once. Twice. Up and down with long then shallow strokes, finding a rhythm that feels good. My pace picks up as I remember my fantasy of ramming into Ella from behind. Her tight channel milking my cock.

My eyes close as a sexy mental movie plays of Ella in front of me on her knees as I ride her body from behind. Her breasts bouncing harder each time I pound into her back and forth. My breathing escalates and shortens as my strokes become choppy. In my mind, I envision her head turning toward me, looking up at me with longing, lips parted, ecstasy written on her face.

"Fuck!" I'm lost. My spine tingles as I continue to pump my cock. My balls draw up tight as the sensation of her pussy squeezing me sends me over the abyss. I come hard, finding my release. I lean against the wall for a few minutes until my breathing is normal. It's over just as fast as it began and unfulfilling because she's not here. My body is reacting to the powerful connection we shared so many years ago. There's never been a doubt. She owns me. Body and soul.

CHAPTER 24

Ella

Friday rolls around sooner than expected. I'm caught up in a whirlwind of emotions. Since the moment I left Grayson in the hallway, I haven't been able to think about anything else. I know, I know. Crazy, right?

"Why did I agree to this?" I sigh.

I'm engaged to another man. But Grayson and I have history together. From the very beginning when my family moved to Lakeview, I had my eyes on him, mystified by the boy he was. He sparked a burning in me that could only be quenched by him. Call it a crush or just plain puppy love, I was hooked when we finally became friends...then more than friends. A blush covers my cheeks, thinking about him as I walk into TMC to begin my day. Can I do this? Can I really have lunch with Grayson and just be friends again? *Awkward to the 200th power!*

Leaving Michael this morning rakes on my nerves. Not because of him, but because of me. I haven't told him about Grayson and it is eating me up. And to make matters worse, I've distanced myself from Michael. Not intentionally, but it's like getting a Hershey bar and eating some of it, then getting a most beloved Godiva chocolate, which is your ultimate favorite! *Am I wrong for that?*

Hell, the only person who knows about us in my circle is Savannah, and she hasn't been helping any in the advice department. So I've been left to my own devices to figure out what to do and say to Grayson Blackwood.

Michael asked me again this morning if I was 'alright'. *Shit.*

"Ella. What's going on? You know you can tell me anything, sweetheart. I feel like there's a wedge between us and I don't know why, or how to stop it," Michael appealed to me.

He knows me well. Knows that there's something niggling at my consciousness and I'm not telling. *I just can't. Not yet.*

Pushing away from him caused a burning in my chest.

"Everything's fine, Michael. It's just been a long few weeks."

I had to walk away from him, because I knew if I didn't, I would spill it all, but I'm not ready. Thank God we've been on different shifts this week. Today was the first time we had a few minutes to spare. Once I get my answers, I can talk to Michael. He deserves to know the truth. But Grayson and I have to talk first.

The other thing is the constant feeling of being watched, which is totally wigging me out. I did let Savannah know yesterday during our lunchtime.

"Hey, Vanna. How do you know if someone is watching you?" I asked.

Savannah looked at me as if I'd grown another nose or something.

"What do you mean, being watched, Ella Bella?" Her curiosity was piqued.

"Well, ever since I left the gym last week, I've had this strange feeling I'm being followed. Weird, right?" I continued on, trying to make light of the haunting feeling. "At first I thought maybe it was just Grayson watching me, but nope. I don't think he'd try to scare me. And I know the feeling of his eyes on me." I blushed as I recalled Grayson's attentions. "Anyhoo, it's giving me the creeps. What do you think?"

The concern for me was written all of over her face.

"First of all, if your gut is screaming something's not right, sugar, then it probably isn't. You need to let the security team know that something is off." She pushed that last part as her main point. "We can't be too careful here, Ella. Everyone is on high alert. We'll go to the security office right after work and let them know what's going on. I won't take NO for an answer!"

She finished, and I understood her meaning. Either I did this or she'd do it for me.

"Second of all, you thinking about Grayson more often than not, Ella Bella?" Savannah eyed me with a look that told me she could read me like a book.

I was caught off guard, yet I couldn't lie to my best friend.

GRAYSON
(This Is Our Life #1)

"Well, yes. He's been at the hospital several times this week. I've seen him; he's stopped and talked to me. Not full-blown conversations like the one in the stairwell, yet enough to drive me crazy. And to be honest, I haven't been able to keep him out of my mind." I took a breath. "I just can't help it, Vanna! There are so many answers I need. Things left unsaid between us. Once I have those answers, I'm sure I can move on. Right?" I finished up with a question.

Savannah eyed me skeptically, but then her scowl turned into a smile.

"Well, baby cakes, if that's the closure you need, then yes!"

That's when the convo ended and we had to go back to work. I wanted to talk more about the eerie feelings, but at least now it was out there in the universe.

I'm making my rounds and everything is going normal. It's time for lunch with Grayson. My belly is doing flip-flops; it's a bundle of nerves. *Just lunch, Ella.*

Then I get that creepy ass feeling running down my spine, and I'm scanning the halls, trying to find the culprit. Looking to the end of the hallway, I see several soldiers leaning up against the wall, casually talking to each other. Nothing looks out of the ordinary, and my eyes connect with one of them. A brief moment and then it's over and done, yet it was a little unsettling. Maybe because every single one of the men is a scary-ass-looking soldier. Permanent menacing scowls mark their faces. I shake off the nagging emotion due to my anxiety levels being way above my head. I've been treading water for too long and now I'm drowning. Everyone's a suspect to me right now. I continue down the passageway to the mess hall.

At the end of the corridor, I'm blocked. *Well, this is awkward.* Each one of the men eyes me suspiciously. Like they want to ask me a question or twenty! I try to make my way through the human meat locker to the door.

"Excuse me, guys."

"Ella? Ella Anderson, is that you?"

I turn my gaze, hearing another voice from the past. Leaning up against the far wall is Johnny Smith from home. And right next to him is none other than Pete Fuller.

"Holy Mackerel! Aren't y'all a sight for sore eyes. It's none other than Killer and Johnny Appleseed," I joke and hurry over to both of them.

Taking turns, we hug like the long lost friends we are. Styx hugs me real tight, and I can hardly breathe. Same old Pete!

"Ella, you are lookin' mighty fine in those scrubs, darlin'. And my friends call me Styx now, 'cause I'm dy-no-mite!" Pete wiggles his eyebrows up and down.

Johnny is trying not to crack up as he hugs me, and it feels like old times in the View.

"Isn't this a coninkydink, I'm meeting Grayson for lunch today and y'all all show up here. Hmmm.

GRAYSON
(This Is Our Life #1)

What're y'all doing here anyways?"

"Just following orders, ma'am," Styx replies. "Playing follow the leader. Grayson's our Capt'n."

"That's good to know, boys. Some things never change." We continue to catch up until I notice the time and see I'm late for lunch.

"Shit, boys, I'll catch you later. Good seeing you."

The smells of fried chicken, fresh bread, and cooked veggies assault my senses. As if on cue, my stomach begins growling. *Oh dear.* Food is what I need.

Approaching the line to grab my tray, I see a movement to my right. I turn around and see him. Grayson is walking casually toward me with that shit-eatin' grin plastered on his face. I give him a half-hearted smile in return as he grabs a tray.

"Hello, Bluebird." And we proceed down the line to get our lunch.

As we settle at a table in the far corner of the dining area and close to a window, my nerves go from fluttery butterflies to hair-pulling crazy. The smells of grease and freshly baked bread drift around me, causing my stomach to wretch a little. *I feel like I'm on a first date!* What do I say? What do I do? Having had this chat with myself a hundred times this week, I thought I was ready. Seeing my indecision, Grayson takes the reins and helps me out.

"So...you're a nurse in the United States Army. Um, wow. That's really amazing, Ella. So damn proud of you," he starts our discussion. "I heard about your mom. I really am sorry, Ella. I know she meant the world to you. Wish I could've been there," he ends with a sadness in his eyes that catches me off guard. He reaches over to caress the top of my free hand sitting idly on the tabletop.

"That's okay, Grayson. It was a long time ago. Besides, she wouldn't want me to sit around feeling sorry for myself, now would she? Just like your grandma Matilda, right?"

Realizing what I just said ensues a flood of memories. *Shit.* I move my hand away from his to clutch my napkin.

"Umm...How's life been treating you? What have you been up to, besides getting shot and all." I laugh, trying to make light of the tense situation.

As I look up, I witness a flash of something in his eyes. Pain mixed with *fire*. Shit! Gotta squelch that quickly. Pulling at my collar and clearing my throat, I carry on.

"It seems you went out and conquered the world, your dreams. I'm proud of you too." I take a huge bite of the fried chicken on my plate. Maybe that'll keep my mouth occupied for a while.

We push on through lunch, finishing up the delicious crispy fried chicken, homemade mashed potatoes, and crunchy steamed vegetables. Country cooking at its finest. Well, maybe not quite as good as I remember Grayson's mother's cooking. *Mmmm. Really good.* It's like we picked up where we left off. Grayson telling me a few new jokes he's learned over the years and me listening and giggling. I'm caught up in this stage that belongs to just the two of us. The rightness of being here with him catches me off guard, and my hardened heart cracks a little. *Oh shit! I'm still in love with this man.*

Grayson puts his fork down and settles back into his chair. Crossing his arms over his impressive chest, he zeroes his eyes in on mine. *Here it comes.*

"I meant every word I said in that stairwell, Ella," he pauses and then continues on. "Now that I've found you again...I'm never letting you go." *Oh dear. Shit. Shit. Shit.*

"I just don't understand what happened, Bluebird," he continues. "When I got that letter from you...it crushed me," Grayson says. *Wait, what?*

"What *letter,* Grayson? *You* broke up with *me.*" My blood begins to boil. "Not even two months after you left, *I* received a letter. Two months!" I emphasize my words. "I was heartsick the moment I read it. And then my mom died. It's hard for a person to come back from so much torment and anguish. But I did! I survived."

Getting up from the table, I pause to take a look at him. This was such a silly idea. To play nice with the man who broke my heart.

"Your time is up, Grayson, I have to get back to work."

I move to the trash bin and throw away my trash. My movements are automatic, and I'm left feeling empty. None of my questions were answered, and now I'm sidelined with more questions. His time is up for now. I have to get back to my rounds.

Making my way around the tables in the dining hall, I chance a glance back at Grayson. His head is in his hands. A scene of sorrow plays out in front of me. I want to run to him and wrap my arms around his big, sexy frame, letting him know everything is going to be fine, but I can't. I still need to know more. *What letter? He sent me a letter. This doesn't make sense.*

'Things aren't always what they seem.' Savannah's voice rings loudly in my mind. I realize one thing for sure. I'm not over Grayson Blackwood.

I focus back to where I'm going, and my eyes collide with Michael's.

CHAPTER 25
GRAYSON

I look up when I hear a commotion at the door. Dr. Barnes has Ella backed into the corner, and my instincts react. Jumping up from the table and across the room in a matter of seconds, I wrap my arms around and through the good doctor's arms, holding him back.

"Back off, Barnes," I forcefully shout at him.

From the corner of my eye, I see my men moving in, encircling us, and the crowded mess hall is now so quiet you could hear a pin drop. I look up and catch the tear-stained cheeks and anguished blue eyes of my beautiful Ella. The hurt is etched all over her face.

"Fuck!" *This isn't good.*

My mind is racing a million miles an hour as my heart pounds out of my chest. When it comes to Ella, I'm lost.

I search her face for answers when she whispers, "It's okay, Grayson. Michael and I just need to talk. It's okay. You can let him go. You're not helping. You're only hurting me. Please, leave...just leave now." Ella gazes at me with pleading, determined eyes asking for me to walk away.

Every cell in my body is screaming to stay and protect her. But I can't, she doesn't want me to. With my mind made up, I drop the good doctor's arms and walk out. Leaving behind my heart.

"Shit! This is so fucked up!" I cry out to anyone who will listen.

Making my way down the hallway and out the front door without looking back, I take off in a full sprint. Needing to get away from everything and everyone. Ignoring the shouts from Johnny and Styx. It'll keep for a little while. A hard run will do me some good. Clear my head, a balm to my aching heart. I follow the long, dusty road, pushing my legs to run faster.

I have to figure out what to do about Ella. With other pressing matters at hand, my carefully constructed world is tumbling around me.

Running through streets of the base, I pass by construction and organized training drills while my legs carry me further away from Ella. My mind drifts back home. Reminding me that just like with Ella, life can change in a blink.

"Son, I have some really sad news. Your dad is sick," mom relayed to me over our monthly video conference.

I was still in New York. Ten more days until graduation. "What do you mean sick, mom? You can't come to graduation like you planned? I understand, I do." I let her off the hook by not showing any of the emotions that were raging inside.

"No, no. We wouldn't miss it." Her smile faltered.

*"But we just went to the third appointment this week
and the second opinion that we wanted," she sighed
toward the camera, and her face fell with unshed tears
rushing into her beautiful, brown eyes.*

"Your dad has cancer, Grayson."

*My mom then continued, explaining to me the
experimental procedure that dad had been approved
for. I was stunned. Shocked by the fact that this
powerful man, feared by most, was dying. I couldn't
stop from thinking maybe this was somehow payback or
karma? Fate's way of evening the score for all the
torment he had caused his family.*

I've only spoken to my father a handful of times
since I left Lakeview. My mom and sisters kept me up
on his procedures and well-being. As of now, the old
man is still kickin'. My father came through the cancer
and is in remission. Lucky bastard! He's been given a
second chance.

I've learned over the years to let it go. I can't
change the man he is...he's no longer in control of me.
But I do have power over my own destiny, and that
includes Ella.

Fifty-five minutes later, I'm back in front of TMC,
sweat pouring down my head, neck, and back. My team
is standing at the front, lounging around like we don't
have urgent business to take care of. "Fuck me!" Out
of breath from the push I gave my body, I make my way
to them. Grabbing my side, taking in deep breaths as I

go. I clutch my elbow to give the deep shooting pain in my shoulder a rest.

"Fuck, Capt'n, what's going on?" Beauty asks the question that my whole team seems interested in knowing the answer to. "Where'd you run off to?"

That's the million-dollar question, isn't it? I gaze upon my team, my men. The men I depend on with my life and who depend on me. What can I tell them? I'm a sap? I'm hopelessly devoted to a woman who may never want me in return? Nope. I take control like always.

"Just needed to clear my head. Wanted to make sure this bullet wound," I point at my shoulder, "could handle some running. That's all." I shut down the concerns and questions I see in every one of their faces. For now at least.

"I've got a few things I need to see about. I'll meet you all back at my quarters to go over the new development with Aabdar." I focus on Johnny. "I need you to stay here and wait for me."

"Yes, sir, Capt'n." Johnny nods and turns to lean back against the off-colored plaster building wall, shading his eyes again with his Oakleys.

Beauty gazes over at me as if he wants to say something. I glance back at him, one brow raised, with 'my word is final' face. I hope he knows to keep his mouth shut right now. I don't need any more fuckin' lip from him. There are too many things that aren't adding up. I've got to figure this conundrum out. I can do this.

GRAYSON
(This Is Our Life #1)

Puzzles, cat and mouse...this is what I was born to do.

I head back into TMC, searching for my target. Leaving the men to follow orders. At the nurse's station, I scan the area. Peering around with no luck of finding Ella, I continue my search through the building. As I'm starting to give up on the search, Savannah comes bopping out of a door to the right and stops abruptly when she sees me.

My eyes pin her in her place. I walk forward as she crosses her arms over her chest and commits to a stubborn stare. Battle ready. This isn't going to be easy.

"Hello, Savannah," I begin with a curt greeting that I hope will ease her a bit.

"Captain Blackwood."

She eyes me with aggravation. *Fuck!* Savannah's not going to make this painless. But I can deal.

"Look, I know you really don't know much about me, and I honestly don't give a fuck what you think. But I need to find Ella." I give her the truth, because that's all I have to offer. "Can you please tell me where she is?"

Savannah looks at me with venom in her green eyes. I brace for impact.

"Well, let me just start by saying I do know you, baby cakes. Ella has told me all about you and your games from the past. You need to leave poor Ella be, and mozie on your way. Sir." She spits out the last part with her fists gripped tightly by her side. "Ella already has enough to worry with a stalker and Michael. Not to mention we're in a war zone!" Her face is reddened from the anger she throws my way.

Wait. A stalker? Oh fuck, no! This woman is hell on wheels, and I need control of the situation now! I hold my hands up in a surrendering gesture, surprise and concern bubbling to the surface.

"Whoa. Slow down for one minute. What do you mean by stalker?" Because that's the only thing my brain registered.

Savannah eyes me, sadness and worry written all over her face.

"Well, shitaki mushrooms! Dammit, you got me all upset, sugar," she says. "When she left earlier, I was so upset for her. Shit! I guess the cat's out of the bag."

Savannah then apprehensively relays to me how Ella thinks someone is watching her, following her. She also informs me they were going to go talk to security today.

"I'll handle the security, Savannah. Thank you for telling me about this. I have a lot on my plate right now, but Ella is a priority."

I need to go and make sure that security is aware. I'll talk to Johnny and Styx, bring them in the loop.

"For some strange reason, sugar, I believe you." She peers up at me while she speaks, her eyes slightly softer. "But you can't hurt Ella again. You weren't there to pick up those broken pieces. It wasn't pretty when we met in basic. And it had been several years since you two were together. I won't allow anyone to hurt her like that again. She's good people!"

I swallow tightly, a knot moving in my throat. I did this to her. How or why is still uncertain, but fixing it keeps me going.

"Savannah, not sure what happened in the past, can't change it. But let me assure you of this...I'm not going anywhere. Ever. Again. Now that I've found Ella," I pause to reign in my emotions, "I can never let her go. I'll never give up on us."

After my ranting, Savannah gazes at me suspiciously but relents. "I understand," is all she says.

Satisfied she gets me, I ask, "Can you at least tell me she's ok? Did she leave and go home?"

"Yep, sugar. Ella and the doc left right after your 'lunch'," she replies, using air quotes. Sighing, she looks at me one more time. "It won't be easy for ya, Grayson. Nothing worth having ever is." She walks away without a backward glance.

She's right, and Ella is worth it!

CHAPTER 26
Ella

Michael walks through the front door of our living quarters, slamming it closed as his temper flares from the earlier confrontation in the mess hall. I know he is hurting, but I'm not sure if I'm going to help make the situation better or not. There's a war raging inside my body. My head is screaming Michael is my future, but my heart's yelling louder that I have to give Grayson a second chance to explain his side of our story. I glance up and see Michael staring warily at me, and I know it's time we talk. He's calm for now.

"What was that all about earlier, babe?" Michael asks. "Why were you eating with the Captain, or better yet, why the hell did you let him touch you? You seemed awfully familiar around each other." His eyes are desperately looking for answers from me.

I'm at a loss for words. As I search for the right things to say without hurting the man I've come to know and care deeply for, I realize this isn't going to be easy, fair, or quick. What I have to say will change the outcome of my future, and I'm not sure I want to delve into the abyss just yet, but Michael deserves to know the truth.

I take a deep breath and begin.

GRAYSON
(This Is Our Life #1)

"I knew Grayson when I was younger. We went to high school together. You could say we were best friends for most of the time until the end of his senior year...that's when things changed." I look directly into his saddened eyes and continue. "When he left for college, we made promises to each other, but only a few months later, he sent me a letter saying he had found someone else. I was left hurt and broken. Mom died, we moved, and things just spiraled from there..."

I'm back there once again as my tears begin falling and my shoulders shake from the wrenching sobs escaping me.

The next moment, Michael has crossed the room and his warm embrace begins comforting the woman in me. He knows there's more, and he's giving me the time I need before continuing. He deserves better. Oh yes, he deserves someone better than me. Someone who will never doubt her love. Never cause him pain. Even if things don't work out for Grayson and I, I know that I can't continue living with Michael. I try to shake the feelings of nostalgia from my mind. It's time, and my heart is bleeding with anticipation of the pain I'm about to deliver.

"When I met you...you helped me find a tiny piece of myself that I thought I had lost forever."

I close my eyes tight while my head shifts left to right, trying to escape his stare. "Michael, you made me believe in fairy tales again, and I really believed I could move on. I'm so, so sorry. I just can't do it. I've been so selfish. You need someone to love you unconditionally, and after seeing Grayson again, I know I'm not that person..." My sobs begin again.

Michael releases his hold on me and begins pacing in front of the couch. His head is hanging from his shoulders, and I know I've wounded him. Why is life so complicated? We were happy until Grayson showed up. Am I making the wrong decision?

He locks his hands behind his head and looks down at me.

"I can't let you go, Ella. You're it for me. I can offer you time, if that's what you need, but please...don't ask me to let you go," he pleads.

My thoughts are jumbled up, and I truly want to agree with him, but I can't. It's not right or fair to the wonderful man standing before me.

"I can't..."

He interrupts me, kneeling in front of me. "I'll give you space. Take all the time you need, and I'll be waiting for you, Ella. No questions asked."

Oh god! He's breaking my heart and slowly disarming me from my resolve. Am I crazy? Should I walk away from the life we've built together? The life I've worked hard to establish?

My fingers absentmindedly find the charms hanging around my neck, and I begin caressing the objects. The reminder I need to finish what I've started. I've been given a gift, and turning my back on it would make me regret my actions for the rest of my life.

"You're too good to me, Michael. You'll always hold a part of my heart. But I've made up my mind and I'm not changing it. I know you deserve better than what I can give you, even if Grayson weren't in the picture and...I'm not sure he is."

"Ella, you sound so certain...this isn't like you. Making rash decisions. Quickly changing the course of your life at the drop of a hat. Take your time, babe, think about how good we are together..."

"No."

I won't let him believe he can change my mind. He's taught me to live life with no regrets, and if I don't follow my heart, I will regret it. This much I know for certain.

"I can't watch you be with someone else, Ella, it would rip me apart. I won't be..."

"I'm going to be Ella. Me. Not Michael's fiancée or Grayson's anything."

"Damn, you really aren't going to change your mind, are you, babe?"

"No. It's made up," I calmly state again. This time with more force in my voice.

"I won't be second to him, Ella, I can't be."

"I know. I'm not asking you to be. I'm just asking you to let me go..." I whisper as I slip his engagement ring off my finger and lay it in the palm of his hand. His fingers close around the ring, forming a fist as he lifts it to his lips. Anguish seethes through his movements as he stands and leaves the room. I hear him in the bedroom, opening and shutting dresser drawers. He's packing.

Moments later, he's back holding his bag.

"I'm going to the hospital. I'll put in a request for temporary housing...not sure how long it will take, but I'm sure I can bunk with Steve, if necessary...see you around, Ella." And then he's gone.

Quiet surrounds the room as I drop to my knees on the carpet and cry. Cry for the pain I've put Michael through. Cry for the loss of the wonderful man and friend he's been to me the past years. Cry because I know he deserves someone who will love him with all her heart. And then I cry because I'm utterly terrified of what's to come...

GRAYSON

Johnny and I leave the security shack and head straight to Ella's. I continue to fill him in on the way there.

"Ella thinks she's being watched. I haven't heard it from her, but to hear it from Savannah, she's scared shitless. We've got to keep an eye on her. Nothing can happen to her, man. You, of all people, know what I'm saying. She's important."

"You always were inseparable. Never could understand what happened between you two," Johnny ponders. "She moved after her mom died, and we all lost track of her. Like she vanished off the face of the earth and didn't want to be found. So weird, man."

"I tried, but like you said, she disappeared. She told me that I sent her a letter. Not sure what the fuck that's about, but I plan on finding out real soon."

Saying it out loud has me questioning this letter more and more. I was stunned at first when she accused me of sending a letter, but the more I think about it, the more I know she was genuinely upset and believed what she was saying to me. I go back to a conversation I had with my dad before I left for college.

"She will never carry the Blackwood name, Grayson, never! Not as long as I'm alive!" my father shouted at me.

I had just arrived from taking Ella home, and he was at it again. He didn't approve of Ella, but the rest of my family loved her. Even though his temper had settled down lately, he still managed to go off at the slightest things.

"She doesn't have the pedigree. Not from good stock, son, and I'll do whatever it takes to make sure of that. You can bank on it." He was calmer and breathing heavily. He turned and sats back in the recliner.

The way things are looking now, he kept good on his word about keeping us apart...my fucking father!

"Motherfucker!" I yell. I'm livid. If he were here

right now, I would hurt him. Johnny raises an eyebrow, questioning me, but I shake my head, letting him know I'm not ready to discuss it.

After several deep gulps of fresh air to clear my head, I'm ready to tackle Ella's situation.

"Need a rotation for Ella's security. I know security is planning to watch her, but I'd feel better if we ran this. Any questions?"

Johnny nods his affirmation, and I know things will be taken care of by my friend. My phone starts ringing and I see it's from TMC. "Blackwood here," I answer into the phone and listen as the nurse gives me the news.

Hitting the end button, I update Johnny, "Aabdar is awake and asking for me. Need to head over there. You good here?"

"Yes, sir," he smirks, and I'm headed back to TMC.

CHAPTER 27
GRAYSON

I'm eager to speak with Aabdar. He's the key to unlocking the chaotic web of theories we are chasing. He knows Mustafa's organization and we need his intel. I enter TMC to find Styx and Beauty waiting outside Aabdar's room for my arrival.

"He refuses to let us in," Beauty snaps as I approach.

He doesn't look happy with the situation. Can't really blame him. This situation is beyond fucked up, and the waiting has begun to grate on everyone's nerves.

"I received a call from his nurse. Let me see what's up and I'll brief you when I'm done," I comment. Not waiting for a reply, I knock on his door and enter the room. Aabdar's sitting up in the hospital bed.

"You're looking better," I say in his native language. I'm not fluent, but I can get my point across most of the time. "Heard you wanted to speak to me."

Aabdar glances at the door with a worried look. He seems apprehensive about talking. When he notices my intense stare, he drops all pretenses and answers, "Yes, I requested an audience with you. I also asked for you to come alone. Yet two of your men stand guard outside my door. You have a problem, Captain, and it needs to be discussed privately. Without other ears around."

I'm completely stunned. That son of a bitch is speaking perfect English. The entire time he has understood what we've been talking about and led us to believe he was ignorant of our language.

"Shocked you, have I? Let's just say the same intel you are trying to gain, well, my government is also. I've been in deep cover, trying to break this cell for years."

"Your government being?" I manage to toss out.

"I'm not at liberty to say. We don't have long, Captain, before your troops will become restless," he voices as his eyes narrow on the door again. "Are you aware of what a sleeper is, Captain?"

He shifts his gaze to me, and I notice it's not apprehension like I believed earlier but awareness of his surroundings. I'm seeing him in a different light as a soldier and not a civilian.

"Of course I have knowledge of what a sleeper is, for fuck's sake! They've been popping up all over the world, wreaking havoc on innocent civilians. Pipe bombs in subways and other public transits have been the most vulnerable to their vicious games. What does this have to do with Mustafa and his cell?" I inquire.

"There is one among your..." he begins when a bullet enters through the window, shattering the glass, and buries itself between Aabdar's eyes. Instant death. Blood and brain matter is splayed on the wall. I drop to the floor, searching for cover, as the door bursts open and Styx is firing at the window and dragging my ass out the door.

"What the fuck just happened?" I'm yelling at Styx. "Where the fuck is Beauty?"

I'm panting from the adrenaline pumping through my body. I haven't used my firearm since being shot, and I'm not able to respond like normal. I had grabbed for my pistol when the window burst, but the ache that began rendered me incapacitated for that split second. Styx's reaction probably saved me from another hospital stint.

"Beauty received a phone call from an informant and said he would be back later," Styx replies as the MPs arrive on the scene.

I'm stunned again. "Didn't I say to stay the fuck here?"

"Yes, sir," Styx agrees quickly.

"We've got problems. Big problems. We're going hunting, Pete, hunting for a rat," I relay to Styx as we turn to leave.

Aabdar's confession has literally pulled the chair out from underneath me. Now, I'm not only dealing with his death and the ambush on my team, but a sleeper. Dangerous times, and I've brought Ella into the mix.

Ella

Michael hasn't talked to me since that night, except once a few days after leaving. I don't blame him at all. I've seen him checking on patients, passing in the hall, but he just looked at me with sad eyes and smiled. I realize I've broken him.

Now, as I enter the doctor's lounge, Michael approaches me. He wants to talk about us, and once again I have to remind him there isn't an us anymore. We can only be friends.

"Ella, I need to talk to you," Michael says as I start to turn around and leave the room. He is the only one in here, and I'm not in a good place to talk to him. It's still an open wound for both of us, and I don't want to see him hurt. Hiding won't solve anything.

"I'm needed in the OR in fifteen minutes, Michael. Can we talk later?"

"No. I only need a little of your time, babe."

"I'm not your babe anymore, Michael. We've talked. What more is there to say?

"I don't believe you. We're perfect together...you're just confused and need time. I've been thinking...maybe if we left and went back to the States, it would help you clear your mind. We could request leave today. We've been here for almost six months."

"Michael, please...please don't make this harder on

us…"

"I'm not trying to hurt you, Ella. I'm trying to save us. Less than six weeks ago, we were planning our wedding. You and me. We belong. He's your past. We're the future."

Not knowing what to say to him, I turn and leave. What he said is replaying over and over in my mind, but I know my future's not with him. Not anymore. He's on a new path and will find the right person for him. Just not with me. It will take him time to heal, but my hope is he will.

Six hours later, exhaustion has settled into my bones and I'm leaving the OR ready to go home and crash. The soldier we operated on lost both legs from a land mine. It will take months of recovering and more surgeries before he is up and going again. But he will live and that's what matters most. We did all we could to get him set on the right track. I can feel the depression slowly inching its way into my mind as I shake away the cobwebs. I wish I had a tub of cookies 'n cream ice cream right about now to drown out the worries troubling me about my earlier run-in with Michael. I swing the double doors from the intensive care unit open, and leaning against the wall is Grayson. Damn, he looks good as he makes his way toward me.

"Hey, Bluebird, we need to talk. Got a few minutes to spare?" he queries with a grin, showcasing his gorgeous dimple.

I evade his grasp, immune at the moment, and

continue walking. "Not today, Grayson. It's been a rough one."

"I need five minutes. We gotta talk about what happened at lunch the other day. We both need answers. Can't keep running. You belong with me. Sooner or later, we're gonna have to face those questions together."

I stop and give him an about-face, enraged he just won't let the issue go for now. Placing my hands on my hips and giving him my 'I'm not gonna budge' look, I firmly reply, "Yes. I. Can. I said, not today. I've had a shitty one and right now I want a shower and bed."

He's stunned at my outburst and lifts his hands in surrender. Not waiting a minute more for him to say anything else, I turn and continue on my way out. I'm maxed out from dealing with both of the men in my life in one day.

Surrendering to my job has been a blessing for me. After a few more nights of crying for Michael's pain and being scared to death of what the future holds with Grayson, I am ready to go forward. I have to. While trying to get a grip on the things that have transpired over the past week, I walk on autopilot through the hospital. So many feelings have me on edge. I know I did the right thing for Michael and for me. I really don't know where this is going with Grayson, but I know that I can't live with regrets.

TMC is now on lockdown because of the shooting two weeks ago. Damn. My heart hurts thinking about

Grayson right in the middle of all it.

Grayson has been hanging around the hospital on and off this week. *Sigh.* I know he's watching over me. Not that we've had a real sit-down to talk about the elephant in the room. He's giving me space. Time to focus. And if he's not here, Johnny or Pete mysteriously show up. As odd as my life has been lately, it's a welcome distraction. Those creepy feelings of being watched have disappeared too.

I catch a glimpse of Johnny, or Animal as his team calls him, propped up against the far corridor. Dressed in his army fatigues, his bulging arms crossed over his massive chest. Johnny was always a big guy. Now he has filled out nicely. Instead of a boy, a man stands before me.

"How's it going, Animal?" I laugh at the animal part, 'cause it's just so damn funny. Soldiers and their nicknames. "What are you up to today?"

"Just people watching, Ella," Johnny replies as a grin covers his face.

Hmmm. Something is strange about that comment, but I let it go. Like I said before, it comforts me right now.

"Well, I'll leave you to it then. Later, Johnny." Leaving him to his 'watching', I finish up at the hospital and get ready to go home.

A few days later on one of the run-ins with Grayson we decide to have dinner. I sense his eyes on me before I notice him. Grayson is leaning up against the nurses' station desk, staring right at me.

"Bluebird," he nods and without hurrying begins an extensive perusal of me.

Blushing from his intense scrutiny, my body responds in prickles of heat rushing to settle between my legs. I clumsily stammer, "Hi Grayson."

Grayson smirks, knowing the effect he's having on me. He saunters my way, and I take a breath, appreciating the Adonis coming toward me. His powerful legs driving him closer while the standard-issue brown t-shirt caresses Grayson's firm, powerful chest.

He stops and reminds me, "Ella, we need to talk. I'd like to take you to dinner and I'm not taking no for an answer this time."

He's right. This thing between us has been building steadily. These feelings along with the unanswered questions need to be assuaged.

Without further prodding from him, I relent. "Okay, Grayson. But instead of going somewhere, I'm gonna cook for you. What we have to say to each other should be said in private. Let's say my place on Friday."

A broad smile and look of relief mixed with anticipation floods his face. And once again I'm flushed as my belly takes a tumble. It amazes me how he owns my reactions. He is mine. I've known in my heart for a while; now my mind is finally catching up.

"It's a date, Bluebird."

I'm going to cook for him. Yes! Granted, he knows

from our past that I'm not a great cook. But I've learned a few things over the years. So tonight, I'm putting it to the test. Who knows, maybe I'll even surprise myself.

CHAPTER 28
Ella

Exiting TMC, I glance up and lock eyes with him. Grayson is standing at the end of the steps, one arm propped up on a rail. His smile captures me and my butterflies are back.

"Hi." My voice sounds breathless, but in this moment, I don't care. It's what this man does to me.

"Bluebird. How are you today?" His eyes sparkle me to distraction, even when I see the worry on his handsome face. "You still up for dinner?"

I loop my hand through his arm after walking down the steps with a huge smile on my face. We walk in silence to my residence. Enjoying the easy company we share. This feels so right. Two peas in a pod. That's us.

As we come to the front door, Grayson holds out his hand for the key. Releasing it to him, I watch as he opens the door, and we both walk through. Even though it's been a couple of weeks since Michael left this place, having Grayson here feels like I've come home. It's not the four walls surrounding us, but the idea of sharing private moments alone with Grayson away from the hustle and bustle of everyday life.

I'm smiling as I drop my bag on the table. An

honest to god smile. I can't believe we're together at this moment.

The past seven years, I buried all my feelings for Grayson, but he's slowly uncovering each one. Reminding me of the good times we shared. Some skeptics might believe we were too young to feel such intense emotions, but I know they're wrong. When you find the second half of your soul, everything else blends into the background. It doesn't matter your age, color, or race. You become part of something bigger than little ol' you; you become whole.

"You're so beautiful when you smile, Ella."

"Ah, shucks, Mr. Blackwood, you're gonna give me a big head if you keep that up. Make yourself at home while I get dinner going," I reply, casting a saucy smirk his way as I make my way to the kitchen.

Leaving Grayson I busy myself by putting the lasagna in the oven, the one Savannah and I made last night. I'm just buttering up the French bread when I feel his eyes on me. I offer him a drink.

"What would you like to drink, Grayson? I've got water, wine, beer, or if you're in the mood for some of the hard stuff...got that too."

"Beer's good," Grayson replies as he walks over to the fridge and grabs one. He looks back at me. "You want one too?"

"Yeppers," I chime. I'm just finishing up the bread when I feel his arms circle me, and he hands me an ice-cold beer.

"We need to talk. Let's go," he says and grabs my vacant hand, leading me into the living room toward the couch. We take our seats facing each other, and the conversation I've been half dreading, half begging for begins.

"Food smells delicious. When did you learn to cook?" Grayson smirks and takes a long pull from his beer.

I know what he's doing. I see the wheels turning in that gorgeous mind of his. He's trying to make me comfortable. Ease me into opening up, but it's really not necessary.

"Savannah got sick of eating mac and cheese out of a box when she visited." I dive right into delivering the news, "I gave Michael his ring back."

He looks at my ring finger and then says, "You know it never belonged on your hand." He reaches for my finger and gently caresses the blank spot.

"The only ring that belongs here will be put here by me. No one else. Do you understand, Bluebird?"

I'm at a loss for words, but I should have known Grayson would say something like that. He's always known what he wanted and went for it. No holds barred.

"Yes, I understand, Grayson. Just not sure I'm ready to take that step," I mumble.

I'm clearly voicing my own inhibitions. I don't know what I'm waiting for...a sign of some sorts with directions would be nice.

GRAYSON
(This Is Our Life #1)

"I've waited so long for you, Bluebird. It feels like forever," he says as he moves closer to me. We are connected physically and emotionally as he reels me in with his eyes. "Why did you leave the View?"

"My dad came home one afternoon after mom died and said we had to move. I was functioning in a black cloud, so I didn't question why. We moved about forty-five miles away. Then when I left, he moved back. Evan went back with him."

"You weren't there when I came home for the summer. Fuck, Ella, I looked everywhere. No one had even heard from you...thought you just left me high and dry. Didn't realize till the other day that you actually believed I broke things off with a letter. What the hell? You know me better than that. Never would have done something that low. I promised you I would be back. I always keep my promises, Bluebird."

Grayson is getting upset from the memories, and I'm not sure how to calm him now. We need closure from the past, and the only way to overcome the hurt is to face it and deal with it.

"I started college and then decided the army was for me. You know, army strong with all those drills we did in ROTC." Lifting my balled fist to flex my muscles, I begin laughing at the expression on his face. Priceless.

"It was a win-win for me. I left the View and all the, uh, memories and started fresh."

"I got one too, you know, a letter from you telling me it was over. Didn't want to believe you would cut

me off that way, but when I got home, you were gone."
He's staring over my shoulder, reliving the past. He
looks so sad.

"Addie told me you came by the ranch to say good-
bye. Kinda believed you really meant what was written
in the letter then. Cut deep after all we shared."

"What? No...no...no." I'm shaking. What he's saying
makes no sense. Why would he lie? "Grayson, I didn't
send a letter. Not me. You sent one to me. You are the
one that sent a letter saying good-bye. Not me."

He looks at me, and something in his eyes finds the
truth.

"Fuck, knew he did it. Just didn't want to believe he
could stoop so low. I should know better. He's always
trying to control us. Guess he couldn't just let me be.
Nope, he had to go and mess with us. Fuck up the one
thing making me happy."

I'm not sure who's he talking about. It's surreal
viewing Grayson this way. Two sides of a coin. Same
person, so many layers.

"Who, Grayson?"

He sighs and continues, "My father. He told me
before I left he would never accept our relationship.
Guess he found a way to make it happen. You ran away
so quickly, he didn't have to work hard at it."

"I didn't run. My dad moved us," I confirm with
force.

"Semantics, Ella, you could have left your address
with Addie. You didn't."

"I thought it was over."

"Yeah. You gave up that quick."

"I didn't give up. Your letter said you found someone new and it was over," I huff.

"How could you believe that after all..." he pauses and releases a deep sigh. "You should've known. But it doesn't matter anymore. You're here now. We're together."

He pulls me forward into his arms, hugging me tight. I don't resist him. I'm confused. Why would his dad do that?

When he releases me, I question, "Grayson, what are we going to do? So much has happened. It's been so long. It was a lifetime ago."

"What can I say, Bluebird? To me, it feels just like yesterday you were in my arms. That hasn't changed. And if there's even a small chance we can be together, build a life together, well, I don't wanna miss it."

I'm dreaming. Yes, that's what's happening. He's finally here saying all the right words I've wanted to hear for years. I'm afraid that before long, the alarm clock is going to start blaring for me to wake up.

"What about your dad?"

"He won't be a problem. We decide our future, not him." He takes my hand and kisses my palm then maneuvers me until I'm straddling his lap. "You're all I can think about."

"You're really certain, aren't you? I mean, about us? I don't want us to have regrets. I really need to think..."

"You've thought enough, my little Bluebird. It's time to come home," he whispers and captures my lips.

His lips are gentle but firm as he coaxes me into opening my mouth. When his tongue touches mine, all my thoughts center around Grayson and what we are sharing. I'm getting drunk on his taste. My head is spinning, and all the worries from the past are slowly fading away. He's fixing the walls I've erected, building them back with new memories. The possibilities of the future seem brighter.

A moan escapes me when his hand begins to roam closer to my breast. It feels heavenly. I grip the hem of his shirt, trying to inch it up. I need to touch his skin. Before I'm able to touch him, Grayson takes my hands and breaks the kiss.

"I can't live without you, Ella. Don't wanna even try. We're meant. We can play this game...keep fighting our feelings. Chase those fleeting moments to be together, but if you ask yourself, deep down you know this between us is right...we are right. I wanna stay with you, Ella, please say I can stay," he pleads with me to accept his heart. It's in my hands now.

"Grayson. I...I don't want you to leave...don't want this to end and miss our second chance..." I whisper, praying I make the right choice for us. Searching for the right words to say.

"It's your choice, Bluebird. It's always been your choice."

"Stay with me, Grayson, stay and show me what I've missed...hold me, love me, and don't let go...don't ever let go."

We are going to make the best of what we've been dealt. The future is ours. I've been lost without him. He's right. He's home.

I reach out again to touch his heated skin, soothing my fears. I gently gather the ends of his shirt, slowly peeling it up and over his taut skin. When it comes all the way off, I gasp.

"Oh...my...God!" I whisper.

I trace my fingers over the most beautiful tattoo of a mated pair of bluebirds beginning on his right pec and moving across his shoulder. Grayson shivers beneath my touch, causing my body to quake. Leaning down, I kiss the portrait he has branded on him. A stark reminder that Grayson has never forgotten me.

As if a switch has turned on, the floodgates open, and I begin to sob. I cry for all the years lost, for the anguish I've felt because of it, for this man who hurts just as much as I do. I sob openly for this gift of love as my heart sings with each rapid beat. There is no place for worry or denial. At this moment, I realize I've always belonged to this man and he belongs to me.

GRAYSON

I hold Ella for a long while. Dinner is all but

forgotten. I caress her back in slow circles, pouring all the love I feel for this girl, my girl, into every stroke. Soon, her body relaxes and her weeping subsides. She's clinging tightly to my neck. It's time to show Bluebird how much she means to me.

I pull up from the couch and grip Ella firmly. My fingers dig into her delicious ass as her legs wrap around my waist. *Good girl.* Her breathing is panting in and out. I feel the change in her body, the acceptance of what we're about to do. Her head is buried in my neck, her lips are touching, tasting my skin, and a groan escapes me. Walking into the kitchen, Ella clinging to me, I turn off the oven and head for the bedroom. I lay Ella softly on the bed, capturing her lips on the way down.

I take my time savoring her flavor, paying special attention to her long neck, tasting her up to her ear and back down. Her breath catches as I come back to her mouth and imprison her tongue against mine. Time to get her naked.

Gently, I tug her shirt, pulling it up her heated body. I stop as her breasts come into view and seize the rounded mounds peeking out from her red lace bra. Kissing the flesh that's visible. I still when I see the necklace placed between her breasts and finger the charms laid carefully in the place closest to her heart.

"You...kept these." So many emotions occupy my brain as my heart catches up.

"You've never been very far, Grayson," Ella rasps

while she grips my hand in hers.

I lay a kiss on her hand before I remove the shirt up over her head. I nod, seeing the passion and pleasure in her gaze as I unclasp her bra, releasing her breasts and kissing each reverently. I continue down her body, tugging her bottoms off, snatching her panties as I go.

"So beautiful, Bluebird."

I want to say so much, more, but intense bliss covers my throat, while I take in the delicate beauty presented before me.

Every night for seven long years I've dreamed of this moment. Of connecting with my Bluebird. My mate. My zing. My soul. I want to slow down, but damn, my cock is weeping from the foreplay from the past several weeks, and tasting her skin has me in overdrive.

I crawl back up her body, stopping to get lost at her breasts. Sucking, tweaking, savoring. Lifting my head from between her breasts, I lick each nipple slowly, relishing the luscious cherry dessert. Her ample nipple beckons my tongue. Slowly, my teeth graze the tip, causing a moan to escape her swollen lips. My tongue circles over and over, leaving wet caresses. Her back arches, forcing her breasts closer to my mouth. Smiling, I know what she needs as I take her nipple into my mouth, sucking slowly. Taunting her. Her hips begin to move against my cock. Rocking. Fuck, that feels good. She's driving me insane. Nobody has ever reacted to my touch like Ella.

Her body is on fire, and I know before long her mind

will realize what she is doing. I don't want her thinking, only feeling. Needing my touch. Reminding her of perfection. We were made for each other. My fingers begin to trace my wet kisses. I feel her heart pounding against my hand. Her breaths are quicker now. My hand descends to her blazing center, where my fingers delve into her wetness as my thumb plays with her clit. Anticipation is building. I apply pressure and circle her clit up and down, firing passion from her. My fingers enter her hot tight cunt in and out. Her hips begin to buck against my hand as I finger fuck her. She races toward her release. Her mind is lost to the ambrosia only I can give her. Ella's body surrenders as she stiffens. She screams my name. I've waited seven long years to hear her scream.

"Fuck, Ella. I'm over the moon. You are so hot and sexy. I need you." Delirious for a taste of her, I inch down her spent body and lick her once, twice. Wrapping her legs up over my shoulders, I grab her ass with my hands, burying my face in her juices. She grabs hold of my hair, scraping her nails against my scalp. Taking what I'm so willing to give. I begin my delicious assault on her pussy. Feasting on Ella as another orgasm rocks her world. Ella cries out my name again as her body capitulates, shocks and tremors bucking her off the bed. She's ready.

Standing up and licking my lips, savoring her honey, I begin to take off my BDUs. I watch as Ella sits up on her elbows, surveying my every move, devouring me with her sexed-up blues.

"Fuck, sweetheart. You're burning me up. See what you do to me?"

I push my pants down and quickly dispose of them and my boots. My hard cock is proudly on display. I stroke my long, thick erection in my palm. I hear her gasp.

"Damn, Grayson."

Looking up, I give her the smile I know she desires, and chuckle.

"I've missed you. Can't promise this won't be fast, Bluebird."

Leaning over, I grab a condom from my pants scattered on the floor with the rest of our clothes. Tearing it open with my teeth, I slide it on and move over Ella.

"Are you ready to fly?"

"Yes!" I cover her mouth and sink balls deep into her, stifling her plea. Holding still to catch our breaths before we begin to move. Becoming one again. Our second chance.

From the start, she's been mine. My home. My special place. My solace when the world threatened to consume me. The soothing balm for when I needed comfort. Even when we were separated, I knew we would find our way back to each other. Because she's my Bluebird.

F. G. ADAMS

Meanwhile...

Standing outside the house in the dark cover of shadows, gazing through the uncovered window, Bahadar watches closely as the Captain carries Ella through the house. Going out of sight.

He laughs to himself. "This is going to be too easy. Now that we know his weakness, he will do whatever we want." An evil grin is plastered across his face.

Bahadar backs away without a trace and without Animal seeing him. No one will ever know he was there.

CHAPTER 29
Ella

My shift ends, and Savannah is strolling my way. It's our monthly 10k run. We started it when we first moved out of the barracks after boot camp. The discipline required toughens your mind, body, and soul. I've been walking on cloud nine since my night with Grayson. Everything seems so much better now that we are together again.

"Let's change and get our asses going," Savannah puffs. She's not exactly thrilled to run ten miles in the heat, but hey, it's our thang.

I've got my tankini sports bra and running shorts on and I'm ready to tackle the heat. Savannah is mumbling about her shift being so long. She's not in a good frame of mind. She's been distracted lately, and I'm really concerned about her. I know it has something to do with a guy she's been seeing, but she won't say a damn thing to me. We get our survival packs aka souped-up fanny packs, loop them around our waists, and head out.

The sun is beginning its journey, setting in the distance. There's no breeze and the heat is stifling as we start. We circle TMC and pass several soldiers lingering about, their gazes traveling our path. Our rhythm is synced as we pound the pavement. We are almost to the end of the street when a white van pulls up to the curb in front of us. We make to go around, not noticing anything out of the ordinary. I'm almost to the passenger door when an arm grabs my waist and yanks me backwards. I start to scream when a hand clasps over my mouth. There is something on the cloth that is slammed over my mouth and nose. I can't breathe as darkness descends. My last thought is of Grayson.

I'm groggy as my mind begins to clear. I try to move my right arm and can't. What the hell? I try to open my eyes, but am not able to. My mind's alert now as I remember everything. From what I can discern, both my arms and legs are strapped to a chair. My neck is aching, and I know instantly I've been in this position too long. My eyes are covered, so I focus on using my other senses. That's when I hear feminine sniffling and whimpers. I try not to make a noise alerting the person. Where am I?

"Thank god you're finally awake. We're in a shit load of trouble, Ella bug."

What in the world? Savannah? I shake my head, trying to communicate with her, but I can't, there's something stuck in my mouth and all I can get out is a muffled "help me" which of course is nothing but garbled noises.

"I know you don't understand, but the people that took us are bad, Ella, really bad." She's whispering the last part, and I know something horrible is about to take place.

"Whatever happens, don't give up. Remember what we were taught in training. We are survivors and we'll get out of here one way or the other. We just have to survive. That's it, sugar. Got it? I'm with ya, no matter what…" Savannah is interrupted when we hear the sound of a door opening and closing.

A familiar voice comments, "Has our special guest decided to join us yet?"

"Keep your fuckin' hands away from her, you pig!" Savannah threatens.

That's when I feel someone squeeze my breast hard. It hurts, and I try again to scream. As quickly as it started, it ends.

"We are saving you for later, little one," the deep voice promises. "As for your friend, the boys have sampled her already and want more."

Oh god, no! Not my Vanna. Why is this happening to us? I hear a struggle and Savannah's piercing cry echoing down the hall as the door slams shut.

My mind's having problems comprehending the situation we are in. Weren't we just running a while ago? Laughing and joking about bad hair days and dreading running in the heat? How did we get here? The presence I've been feeling had subsided over the past few weeks; not sure if that's because of Grayson or what, but I let my guard down. Now Savannah is paying the price. Before long, Savannah's screams go silent. Oh please, God, let her be alright. Please save us.

The next time the door opens, I only hear the scuffing of boots, a thump from something hitting the floor, and then the door closing again. I wish I could see what's going on. The darkness is beginning to drive me crazy.

As if someone could read my mind, the bindings around my eyes are unraveling. I blink, trying to focus. I'm seeing spots. The room is dimly lit, and there are shadows cast by the lantern in the far corner. The door slams, and I jump, forgetting someone was in the room with me. I look around and notice whoever it was has left. My heart is pounding with terror when my eyes land on the most heinous sight.

Savannah, my precious friend, has been beaten so badly I can barely make out her face. She's lying on the floor, naked. There are so many cuts and bruises, I'm not sure if she's still breathing. Oh god! I moan between sobbing and thrashing my body back and forth, trying to reach her.

I begin rocking the chair from side to side. It's not attached to the floor and moves easily once I get it tilting. I've got to reach her. I throw all my weight on the next rock, and the chair gives. I'm crashing onto my side to the unforgiving concrete slab below. The air is knocked from my body temporarily. I had forgotten about the gag, and it takes longer for air to fill my lungs.

When I'm finally able to catch my breath, I crawl from one side of the room to where they placed her. I inch closer to her and notice her chest is moving up and down. Thank god! She's alive. My arms and legs bleed as I continue to slowly move toward Savannah. The little bit of clothing I was wearing to jog in does nothing to protect me from the rough bumps and edges of the concrete flooring. I'm getting closer to her.

I'm not sure how much time passes before I tire and stop to rest for a moment. She's about two feet from my face. She's still breathing, but she hasn't made a sound or moved. I study her, trying to wear my nurse's hat to come up with a viable diagnosis. Her lips are split and swollen. Someone has used a knife to cut from her clavicle to her pubic bone and then parallel along her chest, giving the effect of a giant cross. There is blood seeping from the long, jagged wound. It doesn't look deep, but I know it has to be painful. There are other smaller knife wounds on her arms and legs. My biggest concern is the internal injuries she's probably sustained.

I need to help fix her injuries, but I can't touch her. I feel so helpless. I'm not sure how long we lie side by side, not touching. But I keep my eyes on her chest, watching her breathe. As long as she's breathing, we still have a chance.

GRAYSON

Ella's gone. Someone took my Bluebird. Styx had been watching Ella from a distance as a van pulled up and took both Ella and Savannah. He tried to get to them, but the culprits had perfected the abduction. In and out within seconds. They were definitely professionals. Security had slacked the past few weeks, thinking the threat had subsided.

"What've we learned?"

I stare at the table in front of me. My team is assembled and searching every nook and cranny for a link to finding the girls. It's been two days since they were abducted. Forty-eight hours and no contact from their captors. I know the longer we don't hear anything, the bleaker it is for them and their future.

"The license plate on the van was stolen. Another dead end," Styx fumes as he stands and prowls the length of the table. "The van was dumped about forty miles due south. They must have switched vehicles."

"There was blood on the floor in the rear," Doc chimes in. "Not much, I'm guessing from a deep scratch. We're running it now in the database to see if we get a DNA match."

Beauty shifts in his chair, "I've spoken to my snitches and nobody's talkin'. Not sure if they're scared or what."

"I've got an algorithm running now on satellite feed for that area and time of day of abduction. If it caught any of it, we will know in the next thirty," Radar mumbles and continues typing on his laptop.

"Whoever it was knew their schedule. Means they've been watching them for a while now," Johnny mentions.

A cell phone goes off, and everyone looks at Beauty as he holds his hand up for silence. "Davis speaking," Beauty answers, and I motion for him to put the phone on speaker.

When he does, my world tilts when I hear her voice. "They want a meeting with Captain Grayson Blackwood. If anyone else comes..." Ella's voice breaks as she starts sobbing, "They'll finish what they started and...and kill us both."

She's cut off from saying anything else, and a disguised voice continues, "Further directions will be delivered to you soon. Don't keep us waiting, Captain."

Then the line goes dead and I'm left feeling more desperate than any other moment in my life.

CHAPTER 30

Ella

I'm not sure how long we've been here. It seems like forever. Savannah still hasn't woken up and no one has come back in our room. I'm aching all over. Hunger and thirst have kicked in, and I want to cry, but there are no tears left. I know Grayson is looking for me. He's had Pete and Johnny trailing me for weeks. We just have to hold on until they find us. I know if anyone can, it will be Grayson.

The lock on the door is moved, and the knob turns as it slowly opens. A young native boy enters the room with his eyes downcast, carrying a pitcher of water. He places it in front of me and slowly begins to remove my gag. I have cotton mouth and desperately want water. My throat aches as I try to talk, but the boy shakes his head no, silently pleading with his eyes for me to remain quiet. He lifts my head slowly and pours a small amount of liquid into my parched mouth. I choke as the cool water slides down my throat and down the sides of my cheeks. We repeat this once more, and then he stands and walks out the door.

"Wait. Please don't leave," I beg as the door shuts and the lock is bolted into place again. I want to cry, but I know it won't change anything.

"Vanna. Vanna. Please wake up. Please talk to me," I plead, but she doesn't respond. She just lies there, occasionally moaning when she tries to move. It's heart-wrenching, watching my best friend suffer this way.

Sometime later, the door is opened and a man wearing a turban covering his face, in order for me not to see his face I would guess, walks in. He motions behind him, and two men similarly dressed but without their faces covered walk in and make their way toward me.

"Stay away," I scream. "Don't touch me." I try to move, but I'm still bound to the chair.

"Hush now, little one. We need you to give someone a message for us," says the larger, disguised man. My chair is set right, and a card is shoved in front of my face. "You will read this now," he commands.

I don't resist and read into a recorder what it says. The tears I thought were dried up start again. I'm petrified as I whisper their demands. I understand their meaning immediately. They want Grayson, and if he doesn't come, it will be bad. They're going to kill us both.

The two men exit the room, while the one who causes my skin to crawl remains. I'm not stupid. I watch him from my peripheral vision as he moves around the room. He's large, bulky in stature. He has piercing eyes. I can't help but feel as if I know him. I'm just too tired, hurt, and scared to figure out how. It isn't long before he squats in front of me and his finger trails from my knee toward my upper thigh. I squirm, but can't evade his touch.

"You're very beautiful. I wonder if you taste as sweet as you look." He leans toward my ear and whispers, "He won't be able to save you. I'll make sure of that, little one. You'll be my new pet. I don't think I'd get bored with you for a long while."

I remain silent, because I know his type. They antagonize you until you snap and then pounce. They want provocation. They thrive on it. He slowly turns and heads for the door, but before he's gone, he leaves with one more promise, "Your friend will die slowly while you watch, tied up, unable to help. This will ensure your obedience in the future." And then he's gone.

I'm left wondering how we are ever going to get out of this mess, praying that Grayson finds us soon. Savannah's life is hanging in the balance. She needs medical care and if I'm to believe the dark voice, she's not going to get it unless we're found or we escape. I glance around the windowless room and know the latter won't happen unless I can get myself released from the bindings holding me.

GRAYSON

I'm leaving the compound building we've used as

our central hub the past few days when Michael approaches me. He's been hot on my tail for the past few weeks, but I've been able to avoid him. After the mess hall incident, I've wanted to put my fist through his face. He's had what's mine, and I'm not good with that one bit. I'm not worried he could hurt me. I can hold my own, but I don't want to see that look on my girl's face again, so whatever I have to do, I'm gonna do it.

"Captain Blackwood!" he yells.

Fuck no! Not gonna deal with him now. I turn and head in the opposite direction, ignoring his shouts. As fate has so cruelly done to me many times in my life, I only make it to the corner before he catches my arm, stopping my forward progress and yanking me to face him.

"Get your damn hands off me now, Lieutenant, or we're gonna have a problem regardless of my best intentions," I calmly relay with a promise of retribution.

He shoves me back and sneers, "Need to talk to you, Captain, and I'm not taking no for an answer."

I continue to stare at him, wondering what the hell my Bluebird ever saw in him. He's the complete opposite of me and obviously doesn't know when to take a hint.

"Not today, Doctor. I'm late for a briefing with the General," I try once again to evade him and start hedging closer to escaping the fiasco that's about to transpire. When his next comment sends me over the edge.

"Just thought you might want my intel regarding the girls, sir," he drawls so casually you would think he was discussing the weather.

I stop in my tracks. My face masks the fury I'm about to unleash. With fire in my eyes, I grab his shirt and pull him forward. He's startled by my actions. I've gained the upper hand needed to slam his chest with my fists as I bring his face closer to mine.

"What the fuck did you say? If you know something and haven't told me out of jealousy, I will kill you, motherfucker," I promise.

He tries to back away, but my hold is firm and I'm not budging until he answers. His body language emits confrontation. He wants a piece of me, and I'm waiting for his next move when he looks down to where my hands are holding him and takes a hold of my wrists, applying a subtle pressure that causes my fingers to slip away from his shirt.

"She's mine too. I care more about her than you will ever know," he wearily states and releases a sigh of pent-up frustration. "Look, we can settle our dispute later. Right now, she's out there and I need her safe. That's your job, Captain. You need to bring her back."

I've calmed some, realizing the sincerity coming from him about the situation and knowing now isn't the time. Finding Ella is, and I need to focus on her whereabouts, not worry about the past I have no control over.

GRAYSON
(This Is Our Life #1)

"It's been a long two days with little sleep. Chasing leads that go nowhere..." That's all he's getting from me during our temporary truce. I don't apologize to anyone.

He shrugs, "My shift ended right before the girls left for their run. I took the back exit and saw your second get into a white van. Might not mean anything, but I heard about the vehicle used to take the girls description earlier and thought every little bit could help." He salutes me and without another word, turns and walks away.

Without a moment to spare, I run back to the compound, looking for Beauty. My mind is running every possible scenario as to why he would be involved. How could someone I've known for years do something like this, and what are his motives? As I enter the conference room, everyone is still sitting around but him.

"Where's Beauty?"

"Said he was following up on a lead and left right after you did," Johnny replies.

"No way!" This can't be happening. All eyes turn and focus on me. "Radar, pull up Beauty's phone tracker. I wanna know where he is."

"Sure thing, boss man." Radar continues typing, "Hmmm something's off. That's not...what the hell? His tracker says he's sitting in this conference room."

Everyone looks at where Beauty had been sitting earlier as I walk to the seat. Sure enough, his chip is attached to it by a piece of gum. I'm not sure if he thought we would find it and just left it as a precaution or what.

"Fuck!"

"Hold on, boss. The satellite feed is ready for viewing," Radar states, and we watch as the video shows two men exit the side of the white van as the girls are running down the road, both wearing turbans that cover their faces.

"Freeze it," I command, coming around the table to the screen. "Go back just a little...stop. Magnify right here." I point to the man with his arms around Ella. His arm is across her waist, and the evidence that arm displays is irrefutable.

"What do you see, boys?"

"Holy Shit!" Styx exclaims, jumping up.

"Damn. That's his tattoo, isn't it?" Johnny says.

"Yeah, that's his tattoo, and the scar right above it takes all doubt out of my mind," I state. "We've found our sleeper, boys." You could hear a pin drop as the ramifications of what I've said permeate the room.

"Now what?" Johnny asks, eyeing me closely.

"He has no reason to believe we know it's him. We wait until he comes back, and then we make our move," I calmly reply.

I know the plan seems simple, but two lives depend upon us not making waves. Beauty's not acting alone in this, and until the girls are with us, we can't act impulsively.

"Radar, if he asks, we couldn't get the satellite feed. Too grainy or something. Animal, I want you shadowing him when he leaves. Make sure you keep your tracker on, so we know where you are at all times."

"What about me?" Styx asks, barely containing his rage.

"You're with me," I note. "We're going to the meeting once it's arranged."

With the plan set, all we can do now is wait.

CHAPTER 31
Ella

Time has no meaning in the dark prison we've been left to suffer in. My thoughts drift to Grayson and the happiness we've found. We've only just found each other again, and to have it end so soon because of the nightmare we're caught in torments my soul. The future I had always dreamed of is right at my fingertips, only to be cut short by the actions of insane men. Soldiers fighting their holy war against the world in the name of Mohammed.

I've heard them as they've passed the door on and off for hours. I know there are at least five in the building. I think it's an abandoned warehouse in an unoccupied area of town. There haven't been any traffic noises or planes flying above to clue me in to our location.

My wrists are raw and bleeding from trying to loosen the knots, cause any slack, but the rope is not giving despite my efforts. I've been working on them since the last visit from our captors. The brutality and rape Savannah went through can't happen again. She won't survive it, and if I'm to believe what the masked man said, our only hope is to escape.

I'm jostled from my morbid thoughts when

Savannah's moans fill the room. I look at her face and see her right eye is partially open, staring back at me.

"Oh god, Vanna! You're awake," I softly murmur, scared they'll know she's awake and will come take her away from me again.

"Mmm…you gotta get out of here, Ella…"

I interrupt her. "Can't leave you. Won't. We're in this together. I know Grayson and his team's gonna find us. Just hold on, Vanna."

I look at her, and tears are leaking from her eyes, creating a path of dirt and blood as my own trickle slowly down.

"Not gonna make it, sugar. Go without me," she grunts.

I gasp, realizing she doesn't see me tied to the chair, unable to leave even if I wanted to. She's delirious, and I can only assume her condition has worsened. The hits to her head could have caused a concussion or maybe the swelling around her eye isn't allowing her to focus on my silhouette. I search my memories, wanting to remind her of one that we have laughed about several times over the years.

"Hang in there, sweetie. Do you hear me? You can't quit. You remember bootcamp? Yeah? Hell week?"

That's what we dubbed it, because we were run into the ground and spent most of the time puking our guts out.

"I wanted to quit and give up, but your stubborn ass

wouldn't let me. You got so mad at me for even thinking it, and we weren't even friends yet. Thought ya were a little cray cray that day. Remember those last few miles? Wouldn't have made it without ya calling me out. Well, now I'm returning the favor. We don't give up, no matter what. I've got your twenty, sista."

"You've always been a pain in my ass, you know that, right?" she voices as a grimace forms on her brutalized face. "If I don't make…"

"Shut up, Vanna. We're gonna make it. No more shit talk." I can't even begin to think of my life without her in it. She's not only my best friend, she's every bit the sister I always wanted.

She releases a few short, choppy breaths. "Mmm 'kay. Ella, I'm so cold…tired."

"Sleep, sweetie. Just rest." I watch as her swollen eye shuts and her facial expressions begin to relax.

If I weren't observing her so intently, I would have missed her lips move muttering, "Love ya, Ella bug."

"Love you too, Vanna," I respond.

She drifts off into a fitful sleep. I know she is in excruciating pain, but there's nothing we can do about it. We're alone and vulnerable to the man who has captured us. I once again offer a prayer in hope that someone will find us and save us from the madness engulfing our lives. Hoping someone will locate and set us free from our captors before they are able to keep their promise of death.

GRAYSON

Last night was rough as I lay awake, thinking the worst. My mind wouldn't shut off from all the possibilities Ella and Savannah are enduring. Had someone touched or hurt them? Would Ella once again slip through my grasp, but this time forever? Was fate so fickle that we would never share a future together? Have a family? We've already lost seven years, and realizing I might not ever hold her again is fucking with my head. Vivid images of finding them both dead continued to plague me until I finally gave up on sleep and headed toward the compound to wait for updates from the team and Beauty's return.

When I enter the conference room, Styx and Johnny are sitting there, drinking coffee. By the looks of things, they haven't left at all. The strains on their faces speak volumes. This isn't just our job; it's personal. Ella belongs to all of us, and Savannah belongs to Ella, so that makes her part of our family.

"Radar get anything?" I inquire as I pour a cup for myself.

Styx confirms, "Nothing yet. He left an hour ago to get some sleep. He's been tracking Mustafa's movements and thinks they are tied somehow to the girls. Should know something soon."

"What do you mean?"

"He's connected Beauty to several arms shipments.

Looks like our boy's been working with them for some time. He found an offshore account with millions registered to Wayne Davis. Some deposits are around the times we know arms were exchanged. And you know Radar. Once he finds a trail, he's like a bloodhound till he finds what he's looking for. Sure he'll uncover more as he continues his search," Johnny comments.

"Fuck! You tellin' me my girl is being held by that crazy motherfucker?"

Johnny sips his hot brew and continues, "Nothing for sure, but yeah. That's what we're thinking now, and don't forgot Savannah's there too. God knows what's happening to them."

"I will kill every last one of those bastards if they've touched Savannah. No way will they get away from me," Styx vehemently swears as he stands and turns to leave the room. "Going to shower 'n change, be back in thirty."

"What the hell was that about?" I ask Johnny.

Shrugging his shoulders, he replies, "Think he has a sweet spot for her. They've become pretty close friends over the past few weeks."

"I've never seen him act that way about a chick. He's normally not looking for more than one night."

"Don't know, man. But something's different about her for him to act that way."

Our conversation abruptly ends as Jacobs storms through the door, holding a brown envelope in his hand.

The scowl on his face is enough to drown out all other actions. Jacobs's normal tranquil demeanor is gone, replaced by a mask of fury.

He yanks a chair back and plops down before he hastily reports, "Results are in and you're not going to believe what I've learned. Brace yourself, gentlemen. You're about to get the shock of your lives. The DNA we found in the back of the abandoned van is a 99.9% match to Badahur, second in command to Mustafa on the watch list. For years, we've been in the dark. There hasn't been one agency able to get a photo to go with the name. That streak ends today because we've got one now." Jacobs opens the envelope, flinging a picture across the table as he says, "Meet Badahur, also known as Wayne Davis aka Beauty."

"What the fuck! You can't be serious. We know he's involved, but implying he's one of the most wanted men in the world elevates this threat to a new level. I've got to update the General immediately," I note. My anxiety level has spiked. Ella being held by Badadur is my worst nightmare come true.

"Holy shit! How could he have fooled us every day? We've been to hell and back together. He's one of us. Covered my back over and over," Johnny contemplates, thinking out loud.

"I had the lab check the results three times to be sure. I was sick finding out he's been hiding among us. Can't tell you how messed up this is, Captain. I asked the lab tech to hold this news until I reported it to you.

We can't keep this under wrap for long, but with the girls' lives hanging in the balance..."

"This changes nothing with our plan. We have to play his game. It's their only chance." My hands are tied. We can't risk him becoming wise to us. Sitting and waiting isn't something I want to do. The man in love with Bluebird is demanding I storm the fort and rescue her, but the soldier and leader knows the outcome could possibly end without her in my arms, and that's unacceptable.

Doc studies me, and the reflection of conflict I'm fighting is evident when he asks, "What if he finds out? Believes it's a trap?"

I hesitate for a moment. The idea of losing her just when I've found her is brutal, but not acting isn't an option for me. "Can't worry about the unknown. Animal, rally the team. Fill 'em in and then send a message to Beauty. Let's try to lure him out to our territory. Tell him he needs to be at our briefing at zero nine hundred." He nods, pulls out his smartphone, and commences to following my orders.

Couple hours later, we're all gathered around the table, waiting for Beauty to show. My grandmother always told me patience is a virtue, and I'm surely learning this lesson now. Sitting around and not being able to take action is taking a toll on my psyche. My brothers in arms are assembled and ready to go at the drop of a hat. You could cut the air with a knife. Not only are we ready to face one of the world's most wanted men and our fellow soldier, we're ready to save our girls and get the revenge our mind's require.

A ding from my phone notifies me of an incoming email, and I remark it's from an unknown sender. All eyes are focused on me as I motion to Radar, waving my phone in the air. In less than a minute, he's got the email projected onto the screen for all to view. What we see ravages my soul. There's a picture of a dimly lit room with a badly beaten, naked woman lying on the ground in a heap, and beside her bound to a chair is my Bluebird with her head slumped forward. A growl slowly ignites from the pit of my stomach as the scene infiltrates my mind.

Styx slams his fists on the table and shoves his chair against the wall. Johnny and Doc rush over to contain him from destroying all the equipment in the room. His pain is evident, written on his face.

"Calm the fuck down. We've got a job to do, and emotions can't play a part in this rescue mission," I command, looking directly at Styx.

Several minutes pass before he acknowledges me and slowly lowers his arms to his side. When he looks at me, so much is conveyed in a few seconds. Pain, anger, revenge. He's gone into battle mode, and god help the poor sucker who's harmed his woman.

"Boss man, says here you're to go to the coordinates listed and wait for instructions. You've only got thirty minutes to get there to receive the next one," Radar reads. "If you bring anyone or they see a shadow, one of the women will die."

I make the orders, not follow them, and the low-life son of a bitch running this scam is about to find out what happens when you mess with me. "Change up the frequencies we've been using for our trackers. Make us fucking ghosts, Radar. Don't want to give them a reason to hurt them," I command while standing.

I look at Styx. "You in a good enough place to finish this mission?" His face is blank now, all emotion wiped clean, a determined soldier is staring back at me. I'm concerned how it will affect his actions, but don't have time to dig deeper. We need our heads in the game.

"Let's light 'em, Captain," he replies, making his way to the exit, not even glancing back to see if I follow.

"Johnny, need you to be his backup. We know Beauty won't show. He's sent us an invitation to his party, and I'm ready to crash it," I mention as I walk around the large table.

Animal nods. "On it, sir." And I'm no longer concerned about Styx. Johnny's got his back.

"Radar, you're our eyes and ears. Keep me posted as we go. Any signs of hostiles, alert me immediately," I instruct, following Styx's exit.

"Roger that, boss man."

Styx, Johnny, and I gear up for the upcoming confrontation with our nemesis. The image of the girls so worn and helpless will haunt my nightmares for years to come. I'm barely holding it in and am relying on my instincts and training to help get me through the next several hours. I'm not sure what's in store for us, but one way or another I'm going to get my girl and bring her home.

CHAPTER 32

Ella

Hunger and fatigue have settled into my body. We've been left alone, and Savannah hasn't woken again. Her breathing is shallow and she hasn't moved in several hours. Hopelessness and despair plague my waking moments. My neck feels broken from falling asleep in the position I'm in, and delirium is beginning to show in my thoughts. My head weighs heavy on my shoulders and I'm struggling to lift it when the lock slides across the door of our prison and in walks Beauty. My heart begins to beat quickly, because I know he's here to rescue us! Thank god! We're going to be rescued!

Then he greets me and fear consumes every part of my being. "Hello, little one." My mind registers that he's not wearing army fatigues, and the turban on his head isn't part of the issued gear either, causing me to tremble uncontrollably. It's the disguised man standing in front of me. Everything clicks in place, and I realize now what I couldn't piece together before. He's Grayson's second-in-command, and I've seen him with Grayson at TMC a few times.

"You asshole!" I scream. "You did that to her! You hurt her! If I weren't bound to this chair, I would kill you! You coward!"

I continue my tirade, struggling to free myself from the ropes and draining the last of my energy.

He moves about the room with a devilish smirk on his face before stopping in front of me, gripping my cheeks between his fingers and squeezing hard.

"Tsk Tsk, little one. Your temper is unbecoming of your sweetness. You should be careful what you say to me, or your friend will suffer the consequences." He chuckles and releases my cheeks with a flip of his wrist, sending my head in the opposite direction.

"I bet you're asking yourself why would someone like me want do something like this?" he questions and waves his hand in the air. "Is it the thrill of being caught or outsmarting your commanding officers? Hmmm, maybe it's for religious purposes or better yet, maybe I was abused as a child? No...none of those, although they're valid points, yeah? Let me enlighten you, little one...a long time ago, I was approached by a powerful, wealthy man who showed me the path of righteousness paved in gold. Money and power. What more could a man ask for? Oh, the most important...revenge on the founders of Trident Security."

He stops in front of Savannah. "She's breathing still." Then he lifts his leg, rears back, and kicks her in the back, rolling her onto her stomach, eliciting a small cry of pain from the already wounded woman.

"Stop! Please stop! I'll..I'll do anything, but please,

please stop!"

I'm yelling at the top of my voice as he turns toward me and smiles.

"You just did, little one." Then he walks away, leaving the door open.

GRAYSON

I arrive at the checkpoint at exactly the given time. My phone alerts me to a new email with a new set of coordinates to follow. A new picture is attached, and it's worse than the previous one. It's Savannah, and she's being held down by several men while someone is cutting her body. The caption reads, *The little one is next.* My heart is pounding as adrenaline flows. When I find this son of bitch, he's going to suffer a long and painful death. He knew my weakness and is exploiting it.

I jump back on the Harley, following the GPS to the next location checkpoint when Styx's voice rumbles on the com link. "She's in bad shape, Grayson. Doc did a preliminary diagnosis based on the last photo, and she needs immediate care. Broken bones, loss of blood, possible internal damage..."

I understand his concerns. First and foremost our priority is the extraction of the girls and then the possible takedown of the cell's second-in-command, brotherhood style. Once we find their location, it's lights out, motherfucker!

"Boss man, you're coming up on the warehouse district. It's mostly deserted buildings. No civilians. Location should be on your right. Styx and Animal are in position. Sensors are picking up seven warm bodies. Two off to the far right of the complex. Five near the front," Radar reports.

I pull forward, turn the engine off, and kick the stand out. I place the helmet around the handles and start walking toward the only entrance into the building. My palms are twitchy with anticipation. Action towards the abomination I once believed was my friend. That's when I hear her. A gut-wrenching scream. I start to run when Radar comes over the com, "Stop, Grayson. It's a trap. Ella's okay. My feed is showing someone hurting the body on the floor." As an afterthought, he adds, "Must be Savannah." It takes every ounce of discipline not to take off running toward that sound. The sound I know is Beauty's calling card to me.

"Roger that, Radar," Animal says. "Damn, Styx is leaving his position. I repeat he's left his position. Heard what was going down and took off. I can't locate him from my position, but gotcha covered, Cap." Then gunfire erupts around me. Dust kicks up where a bullet ricochets off the clay pavement, and I'm sprinting toward the building for cover. Dodging left to right in a zigzag pattern to avoid being hit. Ducking into the doorway, I let off a few rounds, trying to taking down hostiles as I go. It takes a moment for my eyes to adjust, and I'm firing again, taking down my marks. Three more left to eradicate. I take stock, allowing my senses to control my actions as I make toward the corner the girls are being held.

Animal reports, "Styx has entered the building, Cap."

No sooner has he reported than I hear two shots followed by bellows of pain, and he's by my side, looking for the last culprit, Beauty. I give him a nod and proceed.

"Animal, get down here now. Radar, we're going black. Let's finish this, boys."

I'm ready to hold Ella in my arms. Touch her all over, making sure she isn't hurt and caressing every inch of her body. I want to be the one to console her and help her get past the nightmarish ordeal she's been involved in.

When Animal arrives, we slowly make our way among the pallets, searching for our target. I lead and motion to Styx and Animal to fan out. We approach the doorway from different angles. One of us should make it to them. Styx motions toward an open door, and I know we are almost there when the stench hits me; human waste and blood.

My fear is that he's with the girls, and I dread the upcoming confrontation. We're hugging the wall when I give the signal. I enter the room and take in my surroundings. Beauty is standing behind Ella with a gun pointed at her head. She's draped over his body, providing a shield against my gun. I only have one shot, but I'm not willing to take that chance with Ella's life.

He grins and exclaims, "Checkmate, Capt'n. I win. Place your weapon on the ground and kick it toward me."

I hesitate, and he pushes the gun further into Ella's temple. She yelps, and silent tears freely fall from her beautiful blues. She's looking directly at me, conveying all the love she has in her heart.

"Now, Capt'n. My patience is wearing thin. Me and the missus have places to go, people to see."

I don't want to be without my weapon, but I know my brothers have got my back. I slowly bend down, place my firearm on the floor, and then give it a nudge with my foot to send it in the direction he had said.

"Let her go now. I'm here," I command him with a firm and even tone.

He caresses Ella's chest and smirks at me. "I never said I would allow her to leave with you. We've become really close. I've decided I want her as my pet."

"You'll be leaving here with her over my dead body," I promise, allowing the loathing to filter through my voice.

He shrugs and says, "I can arrange for her to watch your demise. Her training has begun with her friend over there. What's a little more to ensure her obedience?"

I notice Ella, and the look on her face calms me.

She's furious. If she gets the chance, she's going to try something dangerous. Beauty's gun is no longer aimed at Ella. He's slacked his hold during his ranting. Ella shifts and tries to offer a small resistance, causing him to tighten his hold around her waist, which takes his attention off me. It's the distraction needed to get her out of his clutches.

I shift to the right as he lifts the gun and aims it at my chest. His fingers curl around the hammer, and moments before the release, Styx rolls in front of the doorway, landing on his belly, takes aim, and shoots the gun from Beauty's hand. I leap toward him as the gun releases from his grasp. It falls to the floor, firing when it lands, hitting Ella, and she's thrown from Beauty's body, screaming from the impact of the bullet. She's joined Savannah on the cold ground, slumped over and unmoving. My mind shuts off the terror of losing her to focus on eliminating the person who put her in this position to begin with: Beauty.

He holds his hand close to his body, using his left hand to grab the weapon holstered in his boot. Lifting, he aims and fires, missing his intended mark. A loud yelp fills the air when Styx powers off another shot, hitting Beauty in the knee. He collapses to the ground, and I strike. Moving swiftly, I secure the weapon from him and wrangle his arms behind his back. Animal walks up and fastens the handcuffs tightly on his bleeding hands.

"You can't stop us. We're everywhere. You can't

even be sure that I'm the only sleeper amongst you, can you?" he rasps as pain begins to register in his psychotic brain.

He's trying to divide and conquer with his ranting, but his words are falling on deaf ears. My brothers-in-arms gather around as we bind and lock Beauty to the chair, ensuring he will not leave this place until we're ready. I turn to my girl. Jacobs is there and is staunching the blood flow. Her eyes are on me as I make my way.

"Hey, Bluebird."

"Hey, Grayson, I've been waiting for you. Kinda took your time finding me," she jokingly sasses.

"Like hell I did."

She smiles at me, "I never doubted...love you."

I bend down and hold her small hand. Lightly kissing her, I vow, "Love you always, Bluebird."

Duty calls when our moment is interrupted by Johnny. He's returned from helping Styx get Savannah into the waiting van. Jacobs is ready to move Ella now. He's taking them to TMC for care. I'll be with her soon. We've got some unfinished business to attend to here.

"See ya soon, Captain," Ella says as Jacobs carries her from the room.

"You can bet on it, Bluebird."

Momentarily, Styx is back, and the three of us turn to the traitor, needing answers. He's in the same position he forced Ella to be in for two long days. We each share the same expression: fury. Beauty smirks and doesn't quiver under the stare. He's relishing the fact we've caught him and know of his transgressions. He's proud of his accomplishments and doesn't regret what's he's done.

Johnny's the first to approach Beauty. When he's only a few feet away, he slams his fist square into his nose. We all hear the horrible crack reverberate against the walls. Styx is there next, punching him in the gut, taking his breath. He continues until the sound of bones fracturing permeates the air. His fists are bloody when he stops and spouts, "You deserve more, you low-life son of bitch."

Beauty's head hangs from the punishment when I approach him.

"Now who's winning, motherfucker?" I lunge forward, planting the toe of my boot in his crotch. His chair falls sideways to the ground. One more loose end needs to be tied up before we're leaving this hellhole.

I lean forward, snatching his hair and yanking his face closer. "Where's Mustafa's headquarters?"

He looks at me with disdain and triumph, shaking and panting for air, "I'll never tell you."

"You will by the time we're finished," I guarantee.

Several hours later, the intel we needed to finish our mission is complete. "Styx, set the charges," I command, keeping my eyes on the worm in front of me.

"All good, Animal?" I want to make sure we have all we need from the pile of shit in front of me before we leave.

"Yes, Capt'n. Locations check out, and the General has teams deploying as we speak."

Styx returns and hands me the detonator. "Time to go home, boys."

We gather our gear and ready for the vehicle. I glance behind me as Styx yanks Beauty's hair taut, slitting his throat. Garbling noises continue from the dying scum as we exit the hellish prison. Once we're in the Humvee, Animal cranks the engine, while Styx is staring at my hand in anticipation of the fireworks as I lift the detonator and push the button. We drive away as the building explodes.

CHAPTER 33

Ella

One year and a few months later.

Looking across the car, I watch as Grayson grips the wheel with his muscled forearms. My eyes travel to his extensive chest, and I watch his pecs move up and down in fascination. He's gorgeous with a capital G. My man, my everything.

So much has happened. We moved back to Lakeview last year, after the kidnapping. I was honorably discharged and am now working at the hospital as a surgical nurse. Grayson hasn't left the military yet. There are lots of loose ends he's still taking care of. His plan is to be released next year, when his time is up. But he's taken a lot of much needed leave.

His brother-in-law Keagan is working on making him a permanent part of Trident Security, his security firm in the View. They take on missions the military wants to keep out of. Grayson has taken part in several assignments since coming home. He won't tell them yet, but I know he loves it.

Glancing back at my husband, the all-familiar butterflies invade my belly. I don't have a clue where we're going, because Grayson won't tell me.

GRAYSON
(This Is Our Life #1)

"It's a surprise, Bluebird. Just relax and let me take care of you for the weekend. My treat!"

What girl wouldn't be excited about that, right? That's the way it's been this past year. Grayson dotes on me, loves me, and leaves me breathless every chance he gets. Not that I don't reciprocate, because I do. It's magical, a fairy tale with hearts and flowers. And I can't get enough of him.

Gazing out the window, I notice we're on a bridge crossing over the bay. My heart rate spikes as it brings back the memories of prom. One of the greatest times of my life other than the night he proposed.

After I was released from the hospital, Grayson took me back to his place. We didn't get out of bed for a few days. Igniting the need and diminishing the fears that plagued us both. The only time we came up for air was when he got down on his knees and asked me to marry him. It was perfect, like my husband.

I'm lying in bed with my head on Grayson's chest, our legs and arms entwined from our most recent love-making session. He's insatiable! And I love it! Grayson kisses my head and begins to unwind from our embrace.

"Where are you going?"

He separated from the comfort of my arms and got down on his knees beside the bed. My insides were going crazy, not with butterflies this time, but big birds fluttering around, causing me to take deep, long breaths as I waited for his response.

"I spoke to my mother about us. She was so happy, Bluebird." He gazed up at me, his heart in his eyes. "Through her tears and smiles, she told me she had something she wanted to give me." Reaching down to his bag, he pulled out a tiny, black velvet box. My heart was going berserk, waiting for what came next.

"I've dreamed about asking you a thousand times, Ella. I love you with all my soul. You are it for me, Bluebird. Will you be mine forever?"

Grayson opened up the box and pulled out the perfect ring. It's a platinum setting with a round solitaire diamond surrounded entirely by small blue diamonds. I gasped.

"Oh, Grayson, it's so beautiful." I choked up as tears sprung forth from my eyes.

"So are you, Ella. My mom sent this ring to me. She said it belonged to my grandmother. I took it and had the blue diamonds added. Because they remind me of you. Will you marry me, Ella? Will you be my Bluebird forever?"

A week later, we decided to forgo any more mishaps. Not wanting to wait any longer, we went down to the chaplain on base and said our 'I dos'. The only ones in attendance were Johnny and Pete. Dressed in our favorite jeans, we tied the knot, and I've never been happier. Grayson and I became one, legally, to the world.

GRAYSON
(This Is Our Life #1)

Savannah's healing. We talk often. Back home in Texas, she's taking one day at a time. Pete followed her, and I'm still not sure how that's working out. They'll be visiting us in a few months. Being captured and almost dying puts a lot of things in perspective. And the fact she was tortured. I shut those thoughts out. We are survivors, she's gonna be alright.

I glance at Grayson and smile. He senses my eyes on him and quickly looks my way, giving me a panty-melting smile as he brings my hand to his sinful mouth, showering kisses all over my knuckles and my wedding ring.

"I love you, Bluebird."

"And I love you too."

My mind keeps drifting to my good news. I can't wait to tell him. My anniversary gift to Grayson.

We drive in silence for a little while longer until he makes a turn I've dreamt of over the years. I look toward the beautifully landscaped Hilton. Excitement bubbles up inside of me as Grayson parks the car, making his way to open my door. I can't contain the buzz anymore as I leap into his arms. Always ready for me, Grayson encircles his firm arms around my shaking body.

"Oh, my goodness, Grayson. Thank you...thank you...thank you." I kiss his scrumptious lips, eyes, cheeks, and neck. Thanking him for this special gift he's given me.

"Anything for you, Bluebird."

"I can't believe you brought me here. Well, yes, I can. This is where everything changed." I say in awe at the remembrance of this place.

"Yes, it is." It's all I receive for the moment. He grabs my hand as he slings our duffle across his shoulder, ushering me into the lobby.

Following Grayson to the elevators, I'm thrust back to our first time here. Giggling like a little schoolgirl, I lean into him as the doors close.

"Reminds me of something...can't quite remember though." Grayson's dimpled smile is out on display for only me.

Playfully slapping at his arm for the comment, I throw myself into his awaiting arms. Rekindling the passion that burns so brightly between us, the ever-present fire slow and steady, consistently burning. Even all those years ago, still raging today.

As we exit the elevators, Grayson swoops me up into his arms. He slides the key card over the lock and carries me into the room.

I'm struck by déjà vu. It looks just like the first night Grayson and I came together in this very room. Lighted candles and rose petals are scattered throughout. The fragrance in the dimly lit area is sailing over my heated skin. Grayson sets me down beside the bed, focusing on me.

"I always knew you would be mine. The first time I laid eyes on you, Ella, you captured my heart. Even though it took a while to happen. It was worth the wait.

Thank you for being mine." Grayson leans down and kisses me with the devotion of a happy man.

Coming up for air, I answer, "I knew it too, Grayson. It was love at first sight, or maybe puppy love." I sigh. "Whatever it was, it felt real and right. I'm so thankful we found each other again."

I enjoy the drizzle of lips as he continues his way to my cleavage. He begins to lick a path, gathering my shirt and yanking it up over my head. I'm caught up in the delicious sensations brought on by his mouth. He continues to undress me until I'm left in nothing but my blue thong. Grayson's favorite.

"I have a surprise for you too, Grayson." I just can't subdue my happy news any longer.

He stops his ministrations and looks at me while he licks his lips. *He is scrumptious.* I tug at his hand from around my hip and place it over my belly. Grayson stares at me and then down at where our hands are placed over my flat stomach. Up at me, then down again. His handsome face is full of awe and reverence as he gives a nod and begins to smile.

"That's right. We're going to be parents, Grayson. Happy anniversary!"

My tears cascade down my cheeks as Grayson stumbles to kneel before me, caressing and kissing my belly. This is a gift. Another breathtaking moment in our lives. I watch him closely as a lone tear falls from his water-filled, brown eyes. This strong, unbreakable man is showing me how much this means to him.

"I love you, Grayson."

He gazes up at me with his big, amber eyes, expressing his love for me and our baby. He responds in a husky, emotion-filled voice, "I love you too. Happy anniversary, Bluebird."

EPILOGUE
GRAYSON

Eight years later.

For every moment in life there is an action and reaction. For so long, I lacked acceptance from my father. And I wanted an unconditional love, something to call my own. Such is life. We live, learn, and grow. At one time, I thought I would never make it.

Since the explosion and Ella's rescue eight years ago, our life has drastically changed. In those long moments when I couldn't find my Bluebird, I almost lost all sense of honor. I'm just so damn thankful someone up there was watching over me, over us, guiding my moves to bring this beautiful woman back to me. She is my life. She completes me. I will cherish her...forever.

At the present, I am captured in another awesome moment with my family. A place that stills grips my heart as I take deep breaths due to the surreality of how far we have come. I opted out of signing back up for another tour a year after the kidnapping. Keagan brought me into his security company as a partner, like my other brother-in-laws, Ollie and Lukas. We all work together, fighting the good fight. Brothers-in-arms and family.

For the most part, it's become the norm in the family, sharing our lives. Never really was a problem for me and the sisters, or even my mom. Our family has come a long way in healing and letting go of the past.

Even with dear ole dad. He's trying to make right all the wrongs he's created over a lifetime. Maybe cancer was a blessing in disguise, a second chance to love instead of hate. Only time will tell. I took years of abuse from my father and that pain runs deep. He tried to destroy my relationship with Ella. I still haven't forgiven him for losing those seven years. For now, we take it one day at a time.

He came to Ella when we moved back to Lakeview as husband and wife, apologizing for the hurt he caused. That was monumental. I'll never forget what Ella said to him.

"Thank you, Mr. Blackwood." He had requested she call him dad, but she just couldn't let go of the hurt he had caused us and I'm okay with that.

"But it was never your choice, or my choice, or even Grayson's choice. Destiny has a funny way of tracking you down and making you surrender. It's true love, a gift from God for us to be together. Even you couldn't change that."

No truer words have ever been spoken. I was bound to my Bluebird from the very beginning.

I'm standing in the waiting room full of love and

hope, holding my son. Not just the first son Ella has given me, our third son... And he's just as precious to me as our two other boys, Taylor and Andrew.

Proudly, I say to all of my family and friends crowded around, "Everyone, I'd like you to meet Cooper Alexander Blackwood."

My voice is gruff with emotion I no longer need or want to hide behind. I'm a daddy for the third time, and I'm walking on cloud nine. The tears are brimming. The coos and awes I hear manifested by my family make me feel like the tallest man in the world. I am complete. This all came to be thanks to the love and passion Ella has for me, and the love and allegiance my family has always given me, even when I couldn't see it.

This is our life, and I wouldn't change it for anything in the world!

THE END

... or just the beginning ...

About The Author

Hello. I'm F.G. Adams. Let me tell you a little bit about me. I come from a large family and learned at an early age to entertain myself which was mostly done through my imagination and reading. My grandmother was an avid reader and seeing her pick up a book inspired my love and obsession with books.

In the beginning, starting a book blog satisfied that longing, and the desire grew to create my own stories. Bringing my adventures and imagination to life. My first book, Grayson, is book one of five in my This is Our Life series. The series centers around the children of a large family from adolescent years to adulthood. The struggle and angst that they go through growing up and finding their way in the world.

My hope is that you enjoy reading and living the adventures my imagination creates as much as I enjoy the writing journey.

Website:

https://authorfgadams.wordpress.com

Facebook:

https://www.facebook.com/AuthorFGAdams/

Goodreads:

https://www.goodreads.com/FGAdams

Twitter:

https://twitter.com/authorfgadams

Signup for Newsletter:

http://eepurl.com/bRThVb

Pinterest:

https://www.pinterest.com/authorfgadams/

Acknowledgements

First I would like to thank my husband for his endless love and dedication to the writing of this book. I know at times I gave you grief, but you stood by and loved me anyway with a smile and encouraging words. You've been supportive, and pushed me to capture my dream. I love you. To my family and friends, thank you for listening to the long unyielding questions and answers. Giving me advice and your thoughts. I have the best support system ever.

To all the Beta Readers, Michele, Chelly, Jen, Sarah, CJ, Cathy, & Amber. You ladies rock! Thank you.

Julia Goda, my editor, thank you for your patience in this long process of craziness! And to Daryl Banner for his formatting expertise and enhancing my vision. Bre Clark Photography for the outstanding photographs and a cover that is like no other. Thanks Jess Peterson. Of course my cover model, Benjamin Bartholomew with his amazing physique and beautiful spirit! Perfect Grayson specimen.

Thank you to Austin Trahan for the beautiful tattoos and book stamps you created. You are gifted and talented! To Sergeant First Class Shannon Burdine, thanks for the insight into making my military novel more real.

Lastly, I'd like to say thank you to Jordan Marie who paved the way and pushed me when I had nothing left. Mayra Statham for the patience and help when I felt lost. A special thanks to the crazy lady herself, Jessika Klide. Thank you for your patience and your unending questions that you so graciously explained. GoBabyGo! Thanks ladies for being wonderful mentors. You are awesome!

To all the bloggers and readers: thanks for taking a chance on me and reading my book. After all, I wouldn't be here without you!

XOXO
F.G. Adams

Made in the USA
San Bernardino, CA
06 May 2017